The Cost of Loyalty

Lock Down Publications and Ca$h Presents

The Cost of Loyalty

A Novel by *Kweli*

The Cost of Loyalty

Lock Down Publications
P.O. Box 870494
Mesquite, Tx 75187

Visit our website @
www.lockdownpublications.com

Copyright 2018 The Cost of Loyalty

First Edition May 2018
Printed in the United States of America

Lock Down Publications
Like our page on Facebook: Lock Down Publications @
www.facebook.com/lockdownpublications.ldp
Cover design and layout by: **Dynasty Cover Me**
Book interior design by: **Shawn Walker**
Edited by: **Sunny Giovanni**

Stay Connected with Us!

Text **LOCKDOWN** to 22828 to stay up-to-date with new
releases, sneak peaks, contests and more…
Thank you.

Submission Guideline

Submit the first three chapters of your completed manuscript to ldpsubmissions@gmail.com, subject line: Your book's title. The manuscript must be in a .doc file and sent as an attachment. Document should be in Times New Roman, double spaced and in size 12 font. Also, provide your synopsis and full contact information. If sending multiple submissions, they must each be in a separate email.

Have a story but no way to send it electronically? You can still submit to LDP/Ca$h Presents. Send in the first three chapters, written or typed, of your completed manuscript to:

LDP: Submissions Dept
Po Box 870494
Mesquite, Tx 75187

DO NOT send original manuscript. Must be a duplicate.

Provide your synopsis and a cover letter containing your full contact information.

Thanks for considering LDP and Ca$h Presents.

ACKNOWLEDGMENTS

To my Fam (From Anotha Motha) Moshood Biola, you make everything so much easier. I will never never take your genuity for granted. Luh you boi!

Shout out the whole state of Ohio (minus the rodents)

The homie Big D from Shotgun (the world awaits you OG)!

My Man Tre from the Motor, until we link back up (I doubt I'll ever laugh as much)!

To BD Twan and Black from Chiraq (low end or no end)!

To everyone else...Salute!

To the entire LDP team... I have never been a part of a family, so I wholeheartedly appreciate your embracing me with open arms.

To my Cover Designer...They tell ppl not to judge a book by its cover. In this case I hope they do. Gratitude!

To my Editor...You will never know how deeply your feedback to this story affected me. I'm humbled enough to admit it is the solidification I needed. Thank you so much.

Ca$h... Your accomplishments are admirable, Big Homie. I personally know of no other person in your situation who's managed to do what you've done. So, along with heartfelt appreciation for the opportunity, I tip my hat!

A LETTER FROM THE AUTHOR:

Greetings from the other side,

My reason for adopting the Swahili name Kweli was because it defined me in one word; REAL!

With that being said this book is dedicated to all my Kwelis (Kings With Exeptional Loyalty and Integrity) around the world. You know who you are!

To my queens, the female Qwelis. Behind every strong man stands an even stronger woman! I ask what would Barack be without Michelle!?

May the REAL prevail,

Kweli

Kweli

CHAPTER 1

"Oooh *shit*, Faygo!" The light-skinned female loudly moaned while clenching the sheets. "You got that heavy-ass dick all up in my *stomach*, baby." With her knees pushed back by her ears, she was chewing on her bottom lip with an expression of both pleasure and pain as she watched him slide in and out of her hairy pussy.

To prevent himself from busting too soon, Faygo quickly pulled out. "Let me get this shit from the back." He panted as he roughly flipped her over.

On all fours with her back deeply arched, she reached between her legs and guided him back inside her furnace. Then, looking over her shoulder, she challenged him, "Beat this pussy up, nigga."

With the iced-out Jesus piece on his 32-inch chain laying on her back, he gripped her narrow waist and went straight to work. Alternating between long-deep, short-fast, and circular strokes, he was performing as if he was auditioning for a porno.

As beads of sweat dripped from his face, he stared down in captivation at the way her pillowy-soft ass cheeks as they jiggled and clapped each time their bodies collided. Without stretch marks or cellulite, she by far had one of the fattest and prettiest asses he had ever been behind.

"Oooh, shit! Yesss! Keep that dick right there!" She screamed when he went long and deep.

Aw yeah, I got this hoe now. He smiled to himself as he repeatedly withdrew his dick to the tip before ramming it back in. When he felt her vaginal muscles tighten up and her thighs started trembling, Faygo knew it was time to turn up.

Grabbing her hair from the root, he snatched her head from the pillow so he could see her fuck-faces in the mirror, then dug his fingers into one of her soft cheeks, and viciously punished her with short, fast strokes.

SMACK! SMACK! SMACK! SMACK! SMACK!

"Oh, my Goddd!" She cried out as her eyes rolled up into her head and her small round breasts wildly bounced around. "You the fuckin' the sh—"

CRASH!

The motel's front door was suddenly kicked in and a hooded-figure disguised in an army-fatigue 'Jason' mask charged into the room. "Back up outta that pussy real slow," he calmly stated while aiming a cannon-sized barrel directly at Faygo's head.

When their bodies were disengaged, the gunman told him to get down on his knees.

Because the female was no stranger to the streets or its entangling violence, she knew exactly what time it was and quickly lowered her head. She had recently met Faygo at the club and, although he cashed-out for the sexual escapades, he was not worth dying over. So, with her eyes closed, she prayed the gunman was thorough enough to peep game.

While Faygo was not easily shook, his eyes revealed the genuine fear the gunman had instilled in him. It was not that his face was hidden behind the sinister-looking mask, but it was the steadiness with which he held the powerful shotgun. That alone told Faygo that he was not dealing with an amateur.

Bitch! Faygo cursed to himself as his eyes darted toward the chair where he had put his coat. Tucked inside of it was a .40 with a 'ladder' in it. He knew his chances of getting to it now were highly unlikely. Unless...

"Look, my nigga," Faygo began his spiel. "My chain worth twenty-seven thousand, and I got thirty-two-hunid and some change in my coat over there." He nudged his head toward the chair. "Just let me grab it for you real quick and you can be on yo' way."

"Get. On. Yo'. Mutha. Fuckin'. Knees." The gunman repeated in a tone cold enough to send chills through Faygo.

With no choice but to try his luck, he went for the chair.

CHT! CHT!

The gunman pumped a round into the Mossberg's chamber and watched in amusement as he scrambled across the room. When he started fumbling inside the coat, he took aim and pulled the trigger.

BOOOM!

"Ahhhhh!" Faygo screamed in agony as the thunderous discharge hurled him to the floor. Using the dresser to pull himself up into a sitting position, he felt a scorching sensation in his right leg and looked down. What he saw caused him to start hyperventilating.

The deer-slug had blown his leg off at the knee.

CRT! CRT!

The gunman fed another slug into the Mossberg's head as he walked down on Faygo. Stopping within five-feet of the whimpering man, he took one hand off the pump and lifted his mask.

Faygo's eyes widened in surprise. "Juan-Juan," he mumbled in disbelief. He had heard the stories about the young boys' appetite for violence, but because he was a few years older and ranked himself a street veteran, he had made the costly mistake of underestimating him.

"Listen to me, lil' bra," Faygo pleaded as he sat in a pool of blood. "I swear on my shorties I'ma make it right. Just give me a few days."

With a mixture of tears and sweat pouring down his face, he took the Jesus piece from around his neck and tossed it by Juan-Juan's feet. "That's on the house, my nigga," he said with a wave of the hand.

Juan-Juan glared at him through merciless eyes as he purposely stepped on the chain. "Jesus can't save you," he declared, right before he pulled the trigger; splattering the dresser and wall with what was once Faygo's head.

CRT! CRT!... BOOOM!

The third blast punched a fist-sized hole in Faygo's chest. "Bitch-ass nigga," Juan-Juan spat as he stared down at the bloody carcass with contempt.

He then spun toward the female—whose head was still down, even as she shivered uncontrollably with fear—and slammed the butt of the gun on top of her head. When she crumpled to the floor, he slid the gun under the bed and calmly left the room.

While Juan-Juan's initial intention had been to execute them both, he had to respect ol' girl's gangsta. Because the act of killing did not make him nervous to the point where he had tunnel-vision, he had peeped her move and clearly understood the meaning behind it. See no evil. Speak no evil. If she knew and respected the game well enough to follow its rules, then it was only fair that she be rewarded with mercy.

On his way back to the car, an '84 Cutlass, Juan-Juan stopped behind the motel and quickly stripped off the mask, sweat suit and latex gloves. Grabbing a lighter and two small medicine bottles from his pocket, he poured gasoline from one bottle over the pile and set it on fire. He then poured bleach from the other bottle into the palm of his hand and lathered them carefully.

Now dressed in Polo khaki's and a button-up, he casually strolled toward the car, where his right-hand, JBo, sat behind the wheel.

* * *

"I'm telling you, man, these fucking kids of mine are getting more and more expensive," Officer Wharton complained to his partner as they sat at a red light.

"Hey, I totally agree with you, bro," his partner, Officer Debus, replied as he drummed his fingers on the steering wheel.

"It's like, the more I buy 'em, the more shit they want," Wharton continued. "And hell, you know we—"

"Did you see that?" Debus interrupted as he stared at his side-mirror.

"See what?" Wharton repeated, turning in his seat to look back.

"Look like two niggers were in the car that just passed us."

"What the fuck would they be doing this far out at this time of night?"

"I don't have the slightest idea, but we're sure as hell gonna find out."

As Debus was making the U-turn, the radio inside the car suddenly crackled to life. "All available units, this is a code-three response. There's a reported shots fired and possible homicide at the Knight Inn on Heatherdowns and Reynolds."

Upon hearing the motel's location, both officers turned to look at each other. The motel was just around the corner from where two black men were seen driving.

As Debus stepped on the gas, Wharton reached up to activate the overhead lights.

* * *

"Start wipin' this mu'fucka down!" JBo yelled over the Flowmaster's loud rumble. When he had glanced into the rear-view and saw the cruiser making a U-turn, he didn't think twice before punching the gas. "I'ma hit a side street when we get on Nebraska, and we jumpin' out this bitch!"

JBo handled the Cutty like something out of a movie as he weaved in and out of traffic and skidded around corners. And just as he was coming up on Nebraska, a paddy wagon came from out of nowhere and clipped the rear of the car; causing him to spin out of control before the back-end slammed into a wooden utility pole.

As they struggled to regain their senses, Juan-Juan and JBo found themselves staring down the barrels of .40 caliber Sig's. "Put your fucking hands up and don't move!"

After being taken to the hospital and treated for minor injuries, they were transported to the police station and placed in separate interrogation rooms.

* * *

"I'm Detective Spryzak, with robbery and homicide, and I'd like to ask you a few questions."

Slowly lifting his head up from the table, Juan-Juan glanced at the clock and saw that he had been in the room nearly four hours. Already knowing this was part of their so-called psychological tactics, he laid his head back down without even looking in the detective's direction. "I need my lawyer."

Placing his hands on the table, Spryzak leaned his wiry frame toward him. "That man inside the motel room is dead. We've already uncovered some pretty solid evidence, so you seriously consider saving yourself before your buddy in the other room beats you to it. C'mon, Taylor, you know how this shit goes."

"I need my lawyer."

"Listen here, you piece of shit!" Detective Sterling growled at JBo. "Not only do I have an eyewitness, but it's just been brought to my attention that you were caught on one of the motel's cameras. So, you better start talking. 'Cause if I walk outta this fuckin' room, I'm not corning back. And when the judge hands your sorry ass a life sentence, then you'll be wishing you had talked."

With a look of defeat, JBo put his head down and slowly shook it. "Fuck!" He loudly cursed.

Thinking he had finally managed to break the suspect down, Sterling's mouth curled into a triumphant smile. He had been applying pressure for over three hours, and this was the first time JBo had uttered a word.

Sterling took a seat across from him and changed his approach. "Just get it out, kid." He spoke in a gentle tone. "Not only will you feel better afterwards, but you'll be doing yourself a huge favor."

JBo nodded in understanding, then leaned forward. With their faces only inches apart, he whispered, "Suck my dick."

"You son-of-a-bitch!" Sterling exploded as he lunged over the table.

Two officers quickly rushed into the room and intervened. "Come on, Dan, this asshole isn't worth it," one of them reasoned.

Saying that he had himself under control, Sterling shook them off and pointed at JBo. "You're done, cocksucker!" He then told one of the officers to check both suspects' hands and clothes for gunshot residue. Before leaving the room, Sterling paused in the doorway and turned to face JBo with an evil sneer. "We'll see who gets the last laugh."

* * *

While laying in his rack, cursing himself for not plugging old girl from the motel room, Juan-Juan heard something slide under his cell door and quickly hopped up. Through the door's narrow window, he caught a glimpse of a female CO as she was leaving the pod.

Not knowing what to expect, since he had only been in the room a few hours, he bent down to pick up the piece of paper. When he saw the first two words, 'In Silence', he smirked to himself as he went to lay back down. *Real nigga shit.*

By JBo sending the message, he was assuring him that his solidity was still intact, and that he would stand firm against the most pressure a man could ever face— the possibility of catching a life sentence.

As Juan-Juan turned to the wall and closed his eyes, his mind went back to when he and JBo's friendship initially began.

Kweli

CHAPTER 2
2007

"Take them bitches off before I knock yo' soft-ass out!" Darius threatened as he towered over the boy standing in front of him. The boy—whose name was Javonte— had arrived at St. Mary's earlier that day in the latest Jordan's. Darius had been on the prowl since his arrival and finally managed to catch him in a secluded area.

Despite being smaller in size and outnumbered two-to-one, Javonte stood his ground. "You got me fucked up."

Darius moved in closer. "Fuck you say, lil' nigga?" Dark-skinned with short dreads and a full beard, the husky fifteen-year-old was accustomed to others being intimidated by his size and manly appearance.

"I said I ain't takin' off shit!"

Prejudging him off his pretty-boy features— wavy hair, funny-colored eyes, and light brown complexion—Darius had mistakenly sized Javonte up as being an easy target. But as he searched his eyes for a trace of fear and came up empty, he knew he had to think fast.

Chuckling lightly, he turned to his accomplice, Lil' Chris— who was as black as oil with a nappy 'fro and beady eyes. He served as one of his cable-ready hitters. "You hear this shit, lil' bra?" Darius asked, nudging his head at Javonte. "This nigga tryna play us like we some hoes or somethin'."

Young and impressionable, the thirteen-year-old took the bait. "You heard the big homie, bra," Lil'

Chris barked as he stepped forward with balled fists. "Som take 'em off or I'm breakin' yo' shit. Flat out."

Presented with only two options, fight or flight, Javonte took a step back and awkwardly put his hands up. He may not have been a fighter by nature, but he was far from a coward.

Unbeknownst to the three, someone had been in the cut, quietly observing the whole scene. Having saw enough, he intervened before the situation could escalate any further. "Why y'all fuckin' wit' the new nigga?" he called out as he strolled towards them with his eyes locked on Darius. He had been waiting for a reason to expose him.

Startled, Darius quickly spun around. A flicker of fear shot through his cowardly heart when he saw who the voice belonged to. "What's good, Juan-Juan?" He questioned with a nervous undertone.

He answered him with a lightning-fast overhand.

"Ahhhh!" Lil Chris' hollered out as he stumbled back while cupping his hands over his nose, which was leaking by the pints. "I think my shit broke," he cried before turning to run off.

The threat taken out, Juan-Juan then pivoted towards a wide-eyed Darius and snarled. "What, nigga?"

Retreating a few steps to get from within striking distance, Darius glanced over his shoulder at his fleeing partner and the trail of blood he left behind. He tucked his tail and said, "My beef ain't wit' you, lil' bra." Then, he skirted out.

After introducing themselves, Juan-Juan asked Javonte if he wanted to go outside.

He shrugged. "I'on care."

As they quietly sat on top of a picnic table, Javonte was the first to break the silence. "So, how long you been here?"

Juan-Juan stared at the ground for a minute before he answered barely above a whisper, "All my life."

Damn! Javonte thought as he turned to look at him. "How old are you?" He probed further.

"Thirteen."

"Me too!" Javonte smiled. "When yo' birthday?"

"September."

"Mmph." He grunted before mumbling, "Mine November."

Now it was Juan-Juan's turn to smile. "I'm older than you."

"Only by a couple months," Javonte shot back.

"Don't matter if it was only a couple days, I'm still older."

Standing an inch or two taller than Javonte, Juan-Juan had a dark brown skin tone with four long corn rows braided to the back. The lack of any facial hair on his smooth skin would have suggested innocence, had it not been for his eyes. They were deep-set and black, with a piercing stare like that of a young, wild animal. Because it was uncommon for someone his age to possess such cold and callous eyes, it was evident he had seen and endured more than the average teenager.

Juan-Juan suddenly jumped down from the table and told Javonte to do the same.

"Why, wassup?"

"I gotta teach you how to fight, 'cause you was foolin' with that shit you did in there earlier," he joked, causing them both to bust out laughing.

After a couple hours of showing him a proper fighting stance, and a few basic combinations, they were seated back on the table with their elbows planted on their knees from exhaustion. Javonte glanced at Juan-Juan and started to say something, but thought better of it and looked away.

"She didn't want me," Juan-Juan quietly announced. He had caught Javonte's look out the corner of his eye and instinctively knew what was on his mind. And for a reason unknown to himself, he felt a sense of comfort with the boy next to him. "They say she left me at the hospital and never came back." The reflection of pain in his eyes was so raw that Javonte had to look away.

Once the hospital realized that his mother would not be returning for him, Children's Services was contacted. But because he was born addicted to crack cocaine, he was to be kept under the hospital's supervision until he either recovered or succumbed to the sickness that enveloped his abnormally small body.

Seven months later, Juan-Juan defied the predictions of his death and was declared a healthy toddler; subsequently becoming a ward of the state. He had been placed in numerous foster homes throughout his thirteen years, but as a result of anger and anti-social issues, he had yet to find a permanent family.

Javonte then disclosed how he had never met his father and his mother was killed a few years ago. "I ain't ever told nobody, but I saw the whole thing." What he witnessed that night was so horrific that it would forever remain deeply imbedded into his memory. "They never caught the nigga who did it," he continued, "But I'll never forget what he look like."

While the emotion with which he spoke was a clear indication that vengeance would be his if he ever crossed paths with his mother's killer. There was something else that really caught Juan-Juan's attention. It was how Javonte could have easily given the police a description of the man he saw, but had purposely chose not to. His actions suggested that, with him, snitching was forbidden; regardless of the circumstances. That alone spoke volumes in regards to his character.

After his mother's death, Javonte was adopted by his grandmother. Knowing he was deeply affected by the traumatic loss, she smothered him in unconditional love and attention. And just as the nightmares were beginning to fade, her life was unexpectedly taken by a massive heart attack. With no other known relatives to take him in, he was turned over to St. Mary's— a boys-only orphanage.

"Dejuan Taylor! Javonte Bowden!" Standing at the back door with her hands on her wide hips was Ms. Teresa. Rumored to be a lesbian, she was a tall, over-weight black woman who wore her hair cut boyishly short. "Y'all get y'all asses in here right now!" She snapped.

As they slowly made their way toward her, Ms. Teresa positioned herself in the doorway to prevent them from going inside. She narrowed her eyes at

Juan-Juan and pointed a finger at him accusingly. "You better hope I don't find out you the one that hit that boy Christopher." She then turned her attention to Javonte and spoke in a more affectionate tone. "Baby, you too handsome to be hanging around this little evil muthafucka. So don't let him get you in no trouble, you hear me?"

Little did she know, Javonte's loyalty already belonged to Juan-Juan. Besides his grandmother, no one had ever had his back. So, to him, the demonstration Juan-Juan put down earlier was monumental; making him worthy of his genuine friendship. So, like a true comrade, he refused to even acknowledge Ms. Teresa.

When she realized he wasn't going to respond, she grunted and stepped aside. "Take y'all asses straight to bed!"

Because his head was down as he walked past, she didn't see the subtle smile on Juan-Juan's face. He was inwardly pleased by Javonte's display of allegiance.

Later that night, with the covers pulled over his head, Javonte rubbed at his tightly-shut eyes in an attempt to suppress the steady flow of tears. He hated his father for never coming around, he cursed his mother for placing herself in harm's way, and he blamed himself as being the cause of his grandmother's death.

"Am I a bad person, God?" He quietly prayed. "Is that why I lost my momma and my granny, and why my daddy never came around?" No longer able to keep his emotions at bay, he buried his face into the pillow and cried himself to sleep.

The Cost of Loyalty

As the seasons changed, Juan-Juan and Javonte became inseparable. They discussed any and everything, avoided petty arguments, and never disagreed with each other while in the presence of others. And more importantly, they understood and accepted the balance in their friendship; Juan-Juan was the aggressor, while Javonte was the thinker.

One afternoon while they were outside, Javonte suggested that they make a friendship oath.

Intrigued by the idea, Juan-Juan asked him if he had already thought of something.

He shook his head. "Nah, this something we gotta do together."

Because it came from the heart, they finished what would solidify their friendship in a matter of minutes. To ensure that it was ingrained into their minds and hearts, they repeated the oath in unison before going inside for dinner.

"If what I would do for you, you wouldn't do for me, a true friend you couldn't be. 'Cause I'ma carry my friend if he's unable to walk. I'ma speak up for my friend if he's not there to talk. And I'ma watch over my friend until I'm traced in chalk!"

* * *

"I gotta see that nigga, Darius," Javonte announced one morning while they were eating breakfast.

Juan-Juan stopped chewing. "Why, wassup?"

"These niggas in here don't respect me for real, fam." Because of how his run-in with Darius had played out, he knew everyone felt as if he was living in Juan-Juan's shadow. "I know you got   my back and shit, but I gotta be able to stand my own two feet. So, win, lose, or draw, I gotta see that nigga."

Juan-Juan could only nod in understanding and respect.

He blew down on Darius after breakfast. "My nigga want a fair one wit' you, bra."

Eyeing Juan-Juan with a skeptical expression, he bobbed his head. "A'ight, that's wassup." This time, he would have the whole crew in tow. *Let this nigga try some fuck-shit if he want to*, He thought.

When Juan-Juan and Javonte stepped outside after lunch, they were hardly surprised by the large crowd that gathered around in anticipation. They spotted Darius as he stood with his entourage and a look of confidence in his eyes. Because his opponent was smaller, he had already won the fight in his simple mind. He wasn't familiar with the saying, "*It ain't the size of the dog in the fight, but the size of the fight in the dog.*"

Juan-Juan turned to Javonte. "Wassup, my nigga, you ready?"

Javonte nodded.

"Don't try to go head-up with this nigga; he too big. You gotta move around. And when you see an opening, don't stop swinging till that bitch-ass nigga sleep."

Javonte nodded as if he understood, but there was a look of nervousness in his eyes.

"This nigga can't beat you!" Juan-Juan assured him in a forceful tone. "You know why?"

He shook his head.

"'Cause you got something he don't." Juan-Juan then patted his hand over Javonte's chest and barked, "Heart!"

Javonte smiled, the uncertain look now replaced by one of confidence. The crowd formed a circle around the two fighters as they squared up.

Overly confident, Darius rushed in with a leaping left-hook. Unprepared for the wild and sudden attack, Javonte couldn't slip the punch.

"Oooh!" The crowd erupted as he fell flat on his ass.

As Juan-Juan was about to enter the circle, Javonte shook off the daze and hopped back to his feet. He looked at Juan-Juan and banged his fist over his heart. With a smirk, Juan-Juan stood down.

When Javonte squared back up with Darius, he was expecting another knockout punch. So, when he came in with the wild hay-maker, he easily got under it and countered with a flurry of punches. He did not cease fire until Darius was down on his hands and knees. Showing his adversary no mercy, Javonte took a step back and viciously kicked him in the face.

The crowd stood around speechless as the infamous Darius lay face down, unconscious.

* * * *

"I got it!" Juan-Juan yelled excitedly one night as he rose up in bed.

Javonte stopped reading an urban novel and shot him a questioning look. "Got what?"

Only after swearing to remain on their best behavior did the staff allow them to be roommates. Ms. Teresa had voiced her disapproval, but if it meant keeping Juan-Juan under control, the other staff members would have agreed to almost anything.

"I gotta nickname for you," Juan-Juan smiled.

Javonte started back reading.

"Naw, for real though, my nigga. I got something."

"What?"

"JBo!" He stated with emphasis.

Javonte repeated the name to himself several times before he began to nod in approval. He looked at Juan-Juan with a genuine smile and said, "Juan-Juan and JBo."

The co-defendants exchanged a knowing look.

***

Wittenburg then reached back into the bag and pulled out another piece of paper. Laying it on the table for both men to see, he spoke in an apologetic tone. "The bad news is, the feds are picking up your gun case."

Juan-Juan and JBo stared down at the federal complaint in shock.

With the lack of an eye-witness or any physical evidence linking the suspects to the murder, the prosecutor saw the direction his case was headed. They would beat the gun on a technicality, and possibly get house-arrest for the high-speed chase.

Refusing to swallow the bitter taste of defeat, he underhandedly made a call to his friend, Bill Noon, at ATF. "I may need you to pick up a gun case."

Once the prosecutor received a copy of the GSR test, he gave Noon the green light. By sending the case to the feds, he knew a prison sentence was guaranteed.

"Can they really book us for a gun that wasn't even on us?" JBo questioned Wittenburg.

A Ruger P-95 had been found under the hood of the Cutlass. Although both men denied knowing anything about it, it was actually a move they had been putting down for years. It was hidden to where they could stand a basic search if ever pulled over, while at the same time, close by if the call-of-duty suddenly arose.

"Well, technically, they can't prove it's yours or that you had any knowledge of it," Wittenburg answered. "But, you have to consider that the feds do have a ninety-eight conviction rate."

"So how much time you think we looking at?" JBo inquired.

"Because of your prior conviction, to which you both pled out to probation, my guess is between twenty-four to thirty months."

JBo looked at Juan-Juan. Considering what they had actually done, two- and-a-half would be a slap on the wrist.

As Wittenburg was gathering his things, he couldn't help but glance in Juan- Juan's direction. The mentally sharp attorney had not failed to notice his nonchalant attitude after hearing he was cleared on a murder charge. His reaction had only confirmed what Wittenburg suspected from the first time he peered into his soulless dark eyes; that he was a cold-blooded killer.

* * *

Once Juan-Juan and JBo were federally indicted, Wittenburg informed them of the importance in pleading guilty as soon as possible. "By doing so, you'll receive what they call, 'Acceptance of Responsibility', which is a three-level reduction toward your sentence. You factor that in with your 'good-days' and you're looking to be out within eighteen months."

Knowing the chance to be back on the streets by the following year was too sweet to pass up, they readily agreed to take his advice.

As soon as JBo stepped foot back inside his pod, he went straight to the phone and dialed wifey. "I need you to slide down here tomorrow." It was time to check her temperature.

The following morning, he was called for a visit.

Because of excessive drug confiscations that resulted from contact visits, the county jail had recently adopted a non-contact visiting process. For thirty minutes, you saw your visitors on a small TV screen that was encased inside a stainless-steel box with a receiver attached to the side of it.

When JBo sat on the metal stool in front of the TV, he picked up the receiver and the screen blinked on.

"Hi, baby!" Olivia beamed. "I know it's early, but I could hear in your voice last night that you had something on your mind. So, I just wanted to get down here as soon as possible."

Although he appreciated her attentiveness, JBo bypassed the small talk and went straight in. "Aye, look, I ain't 'bout to be gettin' out no time soon. I'm 'bout to cop out to the gun and get eighteen months." He then eyed her closely to gauge her reaction.

Olivia responded without hesitation. "Listen, baby, I know we haven't been together that long, but there's something you need to understand about me. I'm not some weak ass woman who would leave her man during a time of distress. I know it's easier said than done, but I promise you, I'ma step up to the plate and play my position for the next eighteen months. Simple as that."

She spoke with such sincerity and conviction that JBo could only nod in respect. *Damn, this bitch know how to make a nigga feel good.* He smiled to himself.

"And besides," Olivia continued as she lustfully peered down at his lap, "some things are worth waiting for."

"Oh yeah?" JBo smiled. "That's how you feel?"

Her complexion being the color of a Hershey's bar, Olivia had smooth and unblemished skin that didn't require any make-up enhancements. Her weave-less mane, jet-black and wavy, fell near the middle of her back. With seductive brown eyes, Megan Good-like lips that were kept regularly coated in MAC lip gloss, and a smile that revealed pretty white teeth and deep dimples in both cheeks, she had the type of beauty that brought two words to a nigga's mind. Wifey material.

With his mind now at ease, JBo was able to relax. "What you got on?"

Olivia scooted her chair back. Rocking some skin-tight Hudson jeans and a thin Khan's t-shirt, JBo could clearly see the imprints of her thick nipples.

"Lemme see that ass."

After briefly scanning the room to ensure that no CO's were paying attention, she stood up and turned around.

"Mmph, mmph, mmph," JBo said as he slowly shook his head in amazement. "That shit crazy."

Her ass-to-waist ratio could have easily earned her the centerfold in any men's magazine. Standing at 5'4", 135 pounds, with authentic measurements of 36-26-42, Olivia had the type of frame that captivated the attention of both men and women. Hands down, she was the epitome of a bad-bitch.

When the phone beeped twice, signaling that they only had sixty seconds left, JBo leaned close to the screen and stared deep into her eyes. "I need you to hold it down, love."

"I got you, baby," she assured him as she flashed the smile that seized his heart the first time he laid eyes on her.

* * *

While sitting up in his glass ass '72 Chevelle on B's, JBo was at a red light, rocking to the infectious beat of Rich Homie Quan's 'Some Type of Wag', when a convertible 'Maro pulled up next to him. Like magnets, he and the driver's eyes were drawn together. When he greeted her with a head-nod, she responded with a feminine wave and deeply-dimpled smile.

Dimples being his weakness, he paused the music and stuck his head out the window. "Jump in front of me when the light change and pull up in BP."

Not bothering to wait for a response, he leaned back in his seat and pressed play.

When the light turned green and the Camaro slid in his lane, he burned out; the powerful motor causing his back-end to fish-tail.

Whipping up into the gas station, he took up two spaces as he parked next to the Camaro. He opened his door and stuck one foot out while scrolling through his iPad. He found a song to suit the occasion, he then hit play and his four 15's began blaring Lil' Durk's 'Like Me'.

"She'on know about real niggas, she'on know I'm no Boss... she'on know about foreign cars, she'on know what that cost. She'on know about looove, she'on know what that is... she'on know about ridin' around and spending it like this."

In high-top Balenciaga's, a white V-neck and Balmain jeans with a Louie belt, JBo hopped out with his dab on one-thousand.

"Do you make it a habit of flagging women down in traffic?" the driver teased as he strolled up to her car.

"Nah, not for real," he smoothly replied as he stood with his thumbs tucked behind his belt buckle. "But being that I ain't ever seen a woman as gorgeous as you in real life, I had to shoot my shot. And you know," he shrugged, "ain't nothin' to a shot... but a miss."

Impressed by the confident manner in which he carried himself, the driver could only shake her head and smile. "Boy, you something else."

"So, what can I call you, besides gorgeous?" JBo asked with a boyish grin.

"My name is Olivia, but everyone calls me, Livy."

He extended his hand. "I'm JBo."

She quickly snatched her hand back and place it on the gear-shift. "It was nice meeting you, but I should be going."

"Damn, girl, wassup?" JBo questioned, thrown off by her sudden temperature change.

"Please, I'm just not tryna go down that road."

"Down that road?" He repeated with a frown. "Fuck is you talkin' 'bout?"

She hesitated before answering, "I heard about you."

"You heard about me?"

She nodded.

JBo shrugged. "So, what you hear?"

Staring at her lap, she mumbled, "They said you and your friend Juan-Juan be killing people." This was actually something she had recently heard during a conversation between several gossip queens at the beauty salon.

Not easily discouraged from getting what he wanted, JBo laughed at the accusation. "Listen, Olivia. You strike me as a smart woman. So, therefore, you know there's three sides to every story. The side you heard, my side, and the truth. Now, since you done heard one side, it's only fair that you hear my side." He took out his iPhone. "So, put yo' number in here so we can make dinner plans for this weekend, and I'll tell you all about the real JBo. Then, you can decide if what you heard is really the truth."

Struggling with conflicting emotions, Olivia stared at the phone in uncertainty.

"I'ma real one, Olivia. I'm only asking for one chance."

When she reached out and softly took the phone from his hand, a subtle grin appeared on JBo's face. *Got her!*

* * *

On sentencing day, Juan-Juan and JBo received the anticipated sentence.

JBo winked at Olivia as she sat in attendance, then turned to Wittenburg with his hand extended. "It's been real, ol' buddy."

When Juan-Juan and JBo had caught their first case, they learned how worthless a court-appointed lawyer was. While in the county jail, JBo had heard Wittenburg's name mentioned as one of the top lawyers in the Midwest. With his office stationed right up in Michigan, which was only a thirty-minute drive from their hometown of Toledo, Ohio, JBo shot straight up there as soon as he and Juan-Juan got out.

During a free consultation, he explained that he and his friend were neck-deep in the streets and it was only a matter of time before they caught another case. Before leaving Wittenburg's office, he gave him a $3,500 deposit. And every month that followed he would send a money order for various amounts. By the time they caught the body, JBo had sent him a little over $43,000.

As he and Wittenburg shook hands, JBo was glad that he had taken the advice he was once given, that "You ain't gotta get ready, when you stay ready," because he knew that even though their case wasn't that complicated, if they had been represented by a public-pretender, he would have found a way to fuck them over.

When Juan-Juan and JBo were placed in the holding cell to await transportation to the federal detention center in Milan, Michigan, the two friends exchanged a knowing grin.

"We made it, my nigga!" JBo exclaimed as they loudly slapped hands.

"Ain't no mystery," Juan-Juan replied with a devilish smirk.

Unknown to anyone but themselves and God, they had just beat the system on a body once again.

CHAPTER 3

After sitting in the detention center for a month, Juan-Juan and JBo were designated to FCI Manchester. It was a medium-security federal prison situated in the mountainous regions of south-eastern Kentucky.

As soon as they stepped foot on the compound, their first priority was showing their 'paperwork' to their bunkies and everyone from Ohio. Although snitching was now a common practice, they would ensure that their names were placed in a different category.

Determined to get their weight up, they dove head-first into a vicious workout routine. While JBo was motivated by the effect he knew his body would have on women, Juan-Juan was fueled by something totally different— the desire to transform himself into a war-ready machine.

Familiar with the proverbial saying, "Familiarity Breeds Contempt", they stuck to themselves and allowed no one inside their two-man circle. After encountering so many imposters at the detention center, they already knew prison would be no different.

Besides the one incident involving a clown-ass nigga from their city named Pooh-Bear, their bids had flown without any turbulence.

The names 'Juan-Juan and JBo' rung bells throughout the gang-infested streets of Toledo, Ohio. They were known as neutral but vicious young niggas who were shaking a small bag, did it big on occasion, and rumored to have a small graveyard under their belt. The body they just got off on was only gasoline to an already set fire.

Because the lame Pooh-Bear kept his ear to the streets, it was only natural that he would know in advance about them coming to Manchester. So, attempting to make an impression, he put together two big bags of commissary and tried to give it to them on the day of their arrival.

"We good, bra," JBo had told him as the three stood outside in front a housing unit. "We 'preciate you tryna look out, but we ain't in need." Roomie or not, he and Juan-Juan refused to open any unnecessary doors.

Needless to say, the rejection did not sit well with Pooh-Bear. Unable to suffocate his weakness, he allowed a seed of dislike to be planted within himself. And as he watched them spend the limit every month at commissary, cop new shoes and boots, and saw JBo hit the dancefloor every weekend, that seed of dislike blossomed into an even stronger emotion. Envy.

One Thursday afternoon, which is Chicken Day throughout the entire federal system, the chow hall was packed. When Pooh-Bear carried his tray to the Ohio section and saw all the tables were full, he glanced around to see if anybody was done eating and just taking up space. His eyes landed on Juan-Juan and JBo, who were seated next to each other. This was the opportunity he had been secretly waiting for.

"One of you niggas need to get the fuck up!" Pooh-Bear barked loud enough to attract half the chow hall's attention.

Juan-Juan looked around and saw mass people with nothing on their trays. *This nigga pickin' shots*, he fumed to himself.

"You niggas shouldn't be sittin' over here no way!" He loudly continued. "Y'all don't be fuckin' wit' the homies like that." With all eyes on him, Pooh-Bear sat his tray down. "So, like I said, one of you bitch-ass niggas gotta get the fuck up!"

The whole chow hall was now as quiet as a church mouse.

Juan-Juan calmly spun to JBo. "Just chill, my nigga. He can get this seat."

JBo saw through his cool demeanor and shot him a questioning look. Juan-Juan shook his head which meant for him to sit this one out.

"This shit ain't even that serious, bra," Juan-Juan said to Pooh-Bear as he stood up from the table.

"Get the fuck out my way, nigga!" Pooh-Bear snapped. He could already picture himself calling the city, saying, "I had to slap that nigga Juan-Juan in the chow hall today."

When Pooh-Bear went to sit down, Juan-Juan flipped the switch.

CRACK!

The sound of him smacking Pooh-Bear with his tray echoed throughout the chow hall.

As he fell back into some DC niggas sitting at the next table, Juan-Juan grabbed him by his shirt and put him to bed with a vicious right-hand.

While standing over a loudly-snoring Pooh-Bear with a deranged look in his eyes, Juan-Juan decided to make a statement to anyone else who might have thought shit was sweet. He lifted his foot, and a fraction of a second before his Timberland boot would have made Pooh-Bear's ears touch, he was tackled to the floor by one of the dozen CO's that swarmed the chow hall.

As he was being led out in handcuffs, Juan-Juan swept his gaze over the Ohio section and yelled out, "Me and my nigga ain't to be fucked with!"

Those were the most words anyone had heard him speak since he had been on the compound.

* * *

After doing a month in the SHU, which was the special housing unit, and losing forty-one good days, Juan-Juan was let back on the 'pound. Pooh-Bear couldn't overcome his embarrassment and had refused to come back out. He was getting shipped.

Juan-Juan dropped his property off at his room and went straight outside, where JBo was already waiting. After they slapped-up and hugged as if they hadn't seen each other in years, Juan-Juan told him to meet him on the yard when they called the next rec move. "I gotta holla at you 'bout some real shit, my nigga."

He was about to send their lives in a direction he could have never predicted.

"I think I got a way we can get rich," Juan-Juan spoke in a hushed tone as they walked the track.

"How?" JBo instantly inquired.

He went on to explain that while in the shu, he had dreamed about a vicious lick they put down in Columbus. "But this was more than just a dream, my nigga. That shit was like a vision."

As he took in Juan-Juan's solemn expression, JBo had to look away. He could already see where the conversation was headed, and what Juan-Juan had in mind was the exact opposite of what he planned to do when he touched down.

Although JBo maintained his composure while doing his bid, he realized that he was out of his element and prison was not a place he wanted to revisit. To prevent himself from coming back, he knew he would have to learn more than just what the streets taught. It was senseless to think he could continue playing with fire and not eventually catch first-degree burns.

His first step had been to enroll in a GED class. Not one to leave a soldier behind, he urged Juan-Juan to follow suit. "Our whole lifestyle negative, my nigga. We need to put some balance in our shit. So, let's try something different and see where it go."

Juan-Juan rejected the idea without giving it a moment's thought. "I hear you, fam, but that shit ain't me. You already know my motto. *I'ma drop bodies till I drop dead.*"

Despite him being opposed to the idea, JBo went on to get his GED, then took advantage of the free college courses.

Near the end of his first semester, his business management teacher pulled him to the side and gave him the encouragement he needed. "You're a very bright young man, Mr. Bowden. And if you give yourself a chance, I'm quite sure you'll be very successful."

It was then JBo had decided to put the streets on pause and pursue a legitimate career when he got out.

But because he knew his decision would have some type of effect on his and Juan-Juan's friendship, he had been hesitant about bringing the conversation up. He now realized his procrastination had been a grave mistake.

As he was on the verge of telling Juan-Juan he couldn't get involved, he was suddenly struck by a feeling of disloyalty. He began having flashbacks of different experiences they had been through. He knew in his heart that if he didn't help him and something went wrong, he would never be able to forgive himself. *Until I'm traced in chalk, right?* he concluded to himself, recalling their oath.

When Juan-Juan finished telling him the dream, JBo was at a loss for words. "So, what you think?" Juan-Juan asked after a minute of them walking in silence.

JBo turned to face him and grinned, "I think I'ma cop that new RB."

Juan-Juan smirked.

"Fa real, my nigga. The shit on another level, but it's simple." While he had been hoping his dream was so far-fetched that he could talk him out of it, JBo had to admit that after hearing it, he could actually see it happening in real life.

"An' you know what's crazy?" He continued. "My bunky been in the army, so I bet he can pro'ly point us in the right direction as far as that one shit we gon' need."

"I think I know the other two niggas we can use, too," Juan-Juan added.

"Who?" Because the lick in his dream had been carried out by a four-man crew, JBo already knew he was referring to their accomplices.

"T-Woods and Ham."

"Talkin' 'bout them niggas from Cleveland?"

Juan-Juan nodded. "They got it in 'em, bra. And they get out right after us."

Because Juan-Juan had never been much of a talker, he had long ago mastered the technique of observation. He could key in on any street-nigga and, within minutes, determine his caliber. With T-Woods and Ham being in his unit, he had sized them up prior to having the dream. And through their polished manners, he saw two wild dogs which made them perfect for the type of lick that would be put down.

"Yard recall!" The loudspeaker on the yard announced it was time for all inmates to return to their housing units.

"A'ight, look," JBo said as they were walking back. "Holla at them niggas when you go in and see wassup. I'ma cut into my bunky tonight without sayin' too much, and I'll see you at breakfast in the morning."

"Bet."

* * *

Later that night, as Juan-Juan laid in his rack, his conscious would not allow him to fall asleep. For the first time during he and JBo's friendship, he had betrayed his trust. When telling him about the dream, he had intentionally left out the most important part of it— the ending.

Maybe it'll play out different, he thought guiltily as he turned to the wall.

CHAPTER 4

Olivia had been anxiously waiting in the parking lot when JBo came high stepping out the prison's front door. She quickly hopped out and, with her braless breasts bouncing beneath her t-shirt, ran and jumped into his outstretched arms. "Hi, baby!" she sang as she wrapped her legs around his waist and planted wet kisses all over his face.

"What's good, love?" JBo smiled as he held her up by her ass cheeks and effortlessly carried her back across the lot. Courtesy of the weight-pile and mass protein, he was now weighing in at a chiseled 185.

When they reached the 700-horse powered machine she had just copped days ago, he let her down and nodded at the car in approval. *Yeah, this muthafucka tough*, he thought in reference to the Hemi orange Hellcat.

With Olivia's father being close friends with the manager at a Dodge Dealership, she had been one of the first people in the city to come through in a Challenger Hellcat. Her father, Dr. Derrick Patterson, ensured that his only child wanted for nothing. So, when she mentioned the new car, he took her out to the dealership the following day; where she traded in the Camaro and he wrote a check for the difference.

As Olivia gunned the howling engine down the highway, she held JBo's hand while singing along with Beyoncè, occasionally glancing at him. *"I don't know much about fighting, but I'm gon' fight for you. I don't know much about guns, but I've been shot by you. I don't know when I'm gon' die, but I hope I'm gon' die 'bout you. And I don't know much about algebra, but I know one plus one equals two."*

Slouched down in his seat as the Hemi put distance between him and the prison, JBo was staring out the window in deep thought.

Olivia lowered the music and squeezed his hand. "Baby, what's wrong?"

He shook his head. "I'm good." He was actually thinking about Juan-Juan. It bothered him to leave his mans behind. Because if it wasn't for him taking one for the team, he knew he wouldn't even be out right now. *I miss that nigga already.*

Although it was only for a month and some change, this would be their first time being split up since Ms. Teresa put down the foul play at St. Mary's seven years ago.

* * *

As Ms. Teresa witnessed the bond Juan-Juan and JBo developed over a nine-month period, her dislike for Juan-Juan caused her heart to fill with resentment. Placing a call to the director of Children Services, she told her that the two boys had a negative and unhealthy friendship that would likely prevent them from being adopted. "They'll sabotage potential placements just to avoid being separated," she had told her. A week later, she was given permission to make arrangements for their separation.

On the morning JBo would be transferred to a different orphanage, she had Juan-Juan called to the psychology department. She then hurried to their room and woke JBo up. "Get up and get dressed. You got a dentist appointment."

When he looked over and saw Juan-Juan's empty bed, an alarm instinctively went off inside his head. Flashing a sheepish grin, he asked her to give him a second. "I was having a good dream, and need to change my underwear."

"Hurry yo' lil' mannish-ass up!" She yelled impatiently before going to stand in the hallway.

It was then he had quickly hopped up and wrote Juan-Juan a note.

I think they tryna split us up, my nigga. But thanks for everything, especially for being a true friend. And just know that the world ain't big enough to keep us separated.

JBo

When Juan-Juan came back to the room later that morning and found the letter on his bed, he trembled with rage as he read it over and over. Without even giving him a chance to say good-bye, they had taken the only friend he had ever had.

Only knowing one way to channel his anger, he bare-handedly destroyed the entire room. When two security guards came to take him to an isolation cell, he refused to go willingly. His adolescent strength was no match for two adult men, but he gave it everything he had.

As he was being half-carried half-drug down the hallway, Ms. Teresa lurked in the shadows with her mouth curled into an evil sneer.

* * *

4 Hours Later

"I missed this dick so much!" Olivia yelled as she rode JBo backwards in the living room of her condo. With her hands gripping his shins for support, she would slowly lift up, leaving a trail of cum along the way, then slam back down and grind back and forth, and in circles before doing it all over again.

As JBo laid back, enjoyably watching her perform, he was caught off guard when she suddenly hopped up, then spun around and started eating the dick up on some porn star shit. Seductively staring into his eyes as she stroked him with both hands, she was noisily slurping up and down while twisting her head from side to side.

His toes curled when she took him out of her mouth with a loud plop and started sucking on his balls like they were boiled egg-size pieces of candy. "Hmmmm," she hummed as her restless tongue never stopped moving.

JBo felt himself approaching the point of no return and pushed her head back. "My turn," he announced as he flipped her on her back and ate the pussy till she caught the holy ghost and started speaking in tongues. Giving her no time to recuperate, he crawled up her body, eased the head in, then plunged straight to the bottom and made her hit a high-note that would have impressed Mariah Carey.

After several sweaty minutes of doing push-ups in the pussy from various angles, he rolled her on her side. Placing one of her legs over his shoulder, he found a rhythm and started digging. She cried out and tried to run. He snatched her back, put one of his arms around her neck, then locked his hands together and crushed her.

With no way of escaping, she dug her nails into him and screamed as if she was going into labor. "Why are you fucking me like this? You killing me!" When he swayed left and hit her spot, her eyes rolled to the back of her head as she began to have a seizure-like orgasm. "I'm cummin'! I'm cummin'! I'm cummin'!"

His dick soaked in snot, JBo pulled out as her body continued to quiver. "Get that ass in the air."

"Baby, please," Olivia begged as she tried to push him away. "I can't take no more."

Ignoring her pleas, he smacked fire out of one of her ass cheeks and barked, "What the fuck I say?"

Seeing the merciless look in his eyes, she got up on her knees, arched her back, then buried her face in the pillow. As he dove back inside her heated pool, he grabbed her shoulders for leverage and commenced to putting his murder game down. Her ass cheeks jiggled violently as she screamed into the pillow and pounded her fists on the floor.

Barely slowing down, he grabbed the back of her neck and pulled her head up. "You love this dick, bitch?"

"Yesss!"

"You respect this dick?"

"Oh god, yes! Baby, I respect it!"

He leaned down and roughly kissed her, then smashed her face back into the pillow and sprinted toward the finish line.

SMACK! SMACK! SMACK! SMACK! SMACK!

When he felt that unexplainable feeling that signaled he was on the verge of busting, he quickly pulled out and forced every inch of his dick down her throat. And when her tongue slithered out and tickled his balls, it was over.

"Ohhhh shhhit!" He roared at the ceiling as his lower half spasmed and his toes dug into the carpet. After she finished milking him dry, he stretched out on the floor, breathing as if he had just run a marathon. "Gottt-damn, girl."

Olivia curled up into a fetal position as her body continued to tremble.

JBo reached over and affectionately caressed her head. "Wassup, love, you straight?"

She slowly nodded, then, after a minute, opened her eyes and tiredly smiled.

It was a Kodak moment.

After somewhat regaining her composure, Olivia got up and stumbled to the bathroom. She came back minutes later, smoking a Black & Mild cigar; one of the only serious flaws in her character.

Caught up in the moment, JBo fell weak and rolled toward her. "Let me hit that."

She waved him off. "Boy, quit playing. You know you don't smoke."

"Mannn, let me hit that mu'fucka," he insisted. While he and Juan-Juan blew loud-packs and occasionally popped pills, they had agreed to never indulge in tobacco products.

The head-rush he got from the nicotine, combined with the after-effects of busting two back-to-back nuts, turned one toke into several.

Olivia hit his arm. "If you don't pass that back."

Following the second round—where they fucked slow and hard while staring into each other's eyes—they took a bath together before laying in bed watching movies for the rest of the day.

Although he entertained the thought of whether or not she had been loyal during his two-year bid, JBo fought off the urge to question her. That would suggest insecurity on his part, which she could take as a sign of weakness. At the end of the day, all that mattered was that she had played her role without once missing a beat. As for everything else, he would just have to let time reveal the answer.

Olivia suddenly paused the movie and lifted her head up from his chest. "Baby, I want you to meet my father again."

JBo shook his head. "Nah, I'm cool. That nigga on some other shit."

The first time they met, her father could smell the fragrance of the streets on JBo and flat out asked him if he was a drug dealer. Returning the man's stare, he explained that because he wasn't born with a silver spoon in his mouth, he knew what it felt like to not have food on his plate. "So, to make sure that I never experience that again, I do what I have to do to survive." Reading in between the lines, Mr. Patterson asked JBo to leave his home.

"But it'll be different this time," Olivia persisted as she kissed his neck. "You'll be in college and stuff, so I'll be able to convince him that you've changed your life."

With her thriving career as a registered nurse and a good man in her corner, her only goal now was to gain her father's approval of their relationship.

When JBo didn't respond, she rose up on her elbows and looked down at him. "You do still plan to enroll in college and get a job, don't you?"

He looked away and answered, "Yeah, right after me and Juan-Juan handle somethin'."

"Are you serious?" She asked in disbelief. When he opened his mouth to explain, she cut him off. "Listen to me, baby. My love for you is unconditional, and all I want is what's best for you, myself and our future. Can you understand that?"

"Of course, I can understand that. But just let me take care of this real quick, and I swear I'ma do everything I said I would."

Olivia shook her head in defiance. "I know he's your boy and all, but the world doesn't revolve around him." His silent response angered her. "You know what? Just do what you want!" She spazzed before rolling over. "I'm going to bed."

As JBo laid awake that night listening to her light snore, he couldn't help but wonder if he was making a mistake by placing loyalty before something he had always secretly wanted— a woman's unconditional love.

CHAPTER 5
The Following Day

After seeing his PO and getting his license reinstated, JBo had Olivia take him to the storage where she had put his and Juan-Juan's old school cars and other personal belongings. When he got inside the unit, he went to the passenger side of the Chevelle and popped open the inside door panel. Pulling out a small bag, he unzipped it and smiled; feeling instant relief. Inside the bag were rubber-banded rolls of blue faces, totaling close to $24,000— money he had been wise enough to set aside shortly before they got locked up.

Hopping back inside the Hellcat, he leaned over and kissed Olivia's cheek. "Don't stay mad at me, love."

"I'm not mad, Javonte. I'm just concerned. I don't want anything to happen to you."

"It won't. Just give me a minute to handle somethin', then I promise it's gon' be all about us." He kissed behind her ear and sparked tingly sensations between her thighs. "Okay?"

Her eyes closed, she slowly nodded.

"Now let's shoot to the mall real quick," he said as he sat back and fired up a Mild. "I'm tryna grab a couple outfits."

* * *

JBo and Olivia were leaving the mall when he spotted a familiar face heading in their direction. *Look like this nigga done stepped his game up*, he thought as he took in his designer-clothed and jeweled-up appearance.

Feeling someone watching him, the familiar face looked up. When he caught eyes with JBo, his mouth instantly curled into a genuine smile. "JBo, what's good, my nigga?" he called out as he approached him and Olivia.

"What's good, Fat-Cat?" He greeted him as they slapped hands and embraced.

Fat-Cat was the older version of Lil' Chris from the Orphanage. After JBo had publicly exposed Darius outside that day, Lil' Chris finally saw through his facade and fell back. He eventually stepped to JBo on some player shit. "That was my fault, fam," he apologized in regards to the shoe situation. "I was fuckin' wit' a clown." That moment had marked the beginning of a cordial relationship.

"Damn, my nigga," Fat-Cat grinned, "I ain't seen you in a minute. Last I heard, you and Juan-Juan caught a fed bid."

JBo downplayed the experience with a shrug. "We did somethin' slight." He could never glorify doing a two-year sentence when you had men in there knocking down 20's and 30's.

Fat-Cat then introduced the female on his arms as Kiona. Her face basic, she stood at 5'2" with coconut-size breasts, a small fist between her meaty thighs, and a teardrop designed for back-shots.

After JBo introduced Olivia as wifey, Fat-Cat asked him about Juan-Juan. "Where ya' mans at?" It was common knowledge that when you saw one, you usually saw the other.

"He got into a lil' scuffle and they pushed his shit back 'til next month."

"Same ol' Juan-Juan." Fat-Cat smirked as he unconsciously rubbed his nose.

Having coins had enabled Fat-Cat to evolve into a suave ass nigga. The nappy 'fro was now a taper, and the beady eyes were partially hidden behind tinted Carti's. The chief of a small murderous army, he was shaking a mean bag off the pill game.

Before going their separate ways, they exchanged numbers and agreed to keep in touch, with neither man knowing that Fat-Cat would soon put JBo in a position where he would be faced with the hardest decision of his life.

* * *

The weekend and the following week, came and went, then before you knew it, it was time for Juan-Juan to come home. In a rented all white Range, JBo, Olivia, and her girl Tonya— who she had befriended in the past year— picked him up from the bus station in Manchester, Kentucky. They took him shopping at a mall in Lexington, then went to an indoor amusement park, where him and Tonya teamed up against JBo and Olivia in a game of laser tag.

On their way inside, Juan-Juan had been given his first real glimpse of Tonya's body. The chinky-eyed redbone was naturally blessed with the type of measurements a lot of women were taking out a loan to get. She had handful-size breasts that defied gravity, a small waist that flared out into wide hips, and an over-sized but perfectly-rounded ass that shook like it had Parkinson's disease.

From the park—where Juan-Juan and Tonya were declared the victors—they went to eat at Damon's steak house, watched a new-release, then got on the road and made the four-hour trip back to Ohio.

When they pulled up to Olivia's condo out in Springfield township, Tonya grabbed Juan-Juan's arm and waited until they were alone in the truck before turning to him and asking, "You really don't remember me, do you?"

His mind instantly beginning to race, he shook his head. "Naw, you got me confused wit' somebody else. We never met."

"I was the girl in the hotel room wit' Faygo."

* * *

Tonya Marie Hoskins had been around the game since infancy. Having grown up in a home that was a haven for some of the street's deadliest participants, it was considered normal for her to come home from school and find her uncles in the kitchen, water-whipping; with firearms lying around as if they were TV remotes.

While the men in her family did nothing to shield her from their illicit affairs, they did drill the importance of secrecy within her at an early age. "Our last name mean somethin' out here in these streets," her uncles had once told her. "So, don't ever do nothin' to change that." To this day, Tonya had not once violated the code of silence.

"I knew one day I'd get to express my gratitude," Tonya said as she leaned over and kissed Juan-Juan's cheek. "Call it a woman's intuition. And for the record, you ain't ever gotta worry about me speaking on anything to anyone. I come from a long line of wolves, who taught me that there is no such thing as too much pressure."

She then went on to explain how the police had rushed into the hotel room as she was getting dressed and took her downtown for hours of intense questioning. Sticking to her story, she told them she had just met the victim earlier that day and had no information that would lead to an arrest or even a possible suspect. After allowing her to leave, but saying they would be in touch, she caught a Greyhound to Indiana that night and fell off the radar for nearly six months.

"And besides," she concluded with a careless shrug, "that nigga got what he deserved, anyway." The water-mouth type, Faygo had boasted about getting over on Juan-Juan and JBo for a half-a-brick.

As Juan-Juan watched Tonya go inside the house, he knew what had to be done. There was no way he could leave her alive now. She was too close for comfort.

Thinking Juan-Juan was lustfully staring after her, JBo nudged his arm as he walked up. "That's a bad mu'fucka, ain't it?"

He nodded, deciding to keep her confession to himself for the moment. With her and Olivia being close friends, that could allow JBo's heart to cloud his judgement.

"She feelin' you, too, my nigga," JBo said as he unconsciously pulled out a Mild and fired it up.

Juan-Juan cut his eyes at him in disapproval, then looked away.

"It's just a phase, my nigga," JBo said, catching his look. "I ain't gon' smoke these mu'fuckas forever."

Saying he had to make a quick run, Juan-Juan rose up off the truck and walked over to his car— a '72 Coupe deVille, squatting on 26-inch Forgi's, that had jet-black over cocaine-white guts, and the outside resembled death on wheels while the inside looked like heaven on earth.

"You 'bout to go find that bum ass, old-head nigga you be fuckin' wit'?" JBo laughed as he followed behind him.

Juan-Juan wordlessly slid into the car and brought the 472 big-block to life.

JBo opened the passenger door and leaned down. "Don't forget we goin' out tonight," he said, reminding him that he had reserved a VIP booth at a recently opened club called Glass City.

As Juan-Juan pulled off in the Hog, JBo took a deep toke off the Mild before he flicked it and went inside the house. It would have been impossible for him to predict that his newfound addiction would one day affect his life in a way he could've never imagined.

CHAPTER 6

Juan-Juan parked in front of an abandoned duplex and hit the horn three times. For $10 and a fifth of White Rose, his old-head's location had been given to him by a man at the car wash around the corner.

Minutes later, a face cautiously appeared on the side of the house and Juan-Juan lowered his window. Flashing a broad smile, Terry Jones came from between the houses with pep in his step.

From the outside looking in, a person might have considered Juan-Juan crazy for befriending someone like Terry Jones. But beneath the scraggly beard and dirty clothes was a man who not only had a shrewd mind, but one who had also once prevented Juan-Juan from possibly catching a life sentence.

Shortly after Juan-Juan and JBo got split up, Juan-Juan was adopted by a woman named Michelle Davis. Out the gate, she made it clear that her only concern was the monthly check she received for housing him. She rarely cooked, drank like a fish, and brought a different man home almost every night. With no choice but to fend for himself, he started off stealing car radios and selling them to an Arab store owner across the street from the Port Lawrence projects; known as the PL's.

With his bag full of radios, one night he had just finished taking one out of a box Chevy when he was suddenly grabbed by a pair of massive hands. "This my shit you breaking into," a tall, dark-skin man growled. "I should call the police on yo' lil' thieving-ass. Now gimme this damn bag before I change my mind and have you put in jail." Snatching it out of his hands, he began to walk off. "Oooh-wee," the man chuckled as he peered down into the bag and did a little shuffle. "The crack-god is good!" He had been watching Juan-Juan from the moment he threw the spark plug at the Chevy's window.

Realizing he was the victim of a strong-arm, Juan-Juan became enraged. "Aye!" He yelled out after the dope-fiend. "You forgot one!"

Turning around, his eyes got bigger than the rocks he wanted to smoke as he found himself staring down the frightening-size barrel of a .357 Python. Attempting to mask his fear, he took a step forward. "Boy, what the fuck you—"

BOOM!

Lifted off his feet by the chest-shot, he was lying on his back, desperately gasping for air when Juan-Juan went and stood over him; his dick rock hard. He had found his calling. Barely flinching, he fired another shot into the man's face. His body started twitching, which Juan-Juan took as a sign of life, and he fired again.

BOOM!

As blood haloed around the lifeless form while sirens could be heard in the distance, Juan-Juan snapped out of his trance and hurriedly tried to scoop the fallen radios back into his bag.

"Leave 'em!" A voice hissed from behind him.

Startled, Juan-Juan spun around with his arm extended; ready to squeeze the trigger.

"We gotta get the fuck outta here!" the bearded-man urgently whispered before taking off between two houses.

The sirens becoming louder by the second, Juan-Juan reluctantly followed the man's footsteps. They power-walked, but never ran, through alleyways and backyards until the stranger led them inside an abandoned house.

They sat motionless for nearly an hour before the man broke the silence. "I'm Terry Jones."

Regarding him with cautious eyes, Juan-Juan said nothing as he kept his hands inside his coat.

"What you 'bout, thirteen?"

"Almost fifteen," Juan-Juan corrected him, his finger hovering over the trigger.

Terry Jones nodded as if it now made sense. "You hungry?"

Juan-Juan shook his head, but his stomach said otherwise as it growled loud enough to be heard.

Terry smiled in amusement before slowly reaching into his pocket. He took out a Wendy's hamburger and held it out to Juan-Juan.

Unaccustomed to generosity, he stared at his hand for a minute before reaching out and accepting the sandwich. After nearly ravaging it all, he suddenly stopped chewing and looked up with an apologetic expression. He hadn't even offered the man a piece of his own food.

Terry waved him off with a smile. "I gotta another one," he lied. This wouldn't be the first time he had laid down on an empty stomach.

Terry Jones had been on his way home when he spotted the junky lurking in the shadows like a hawk. Not one to meddle in another man's affairs, he kept it moving until he heard the first gunshot. As he witnessed the scene unfold, and foresaw Juan-Juan's outcome, he had instinctively decided to intervene.

He nudged his head at the bag lying at Juan-Juan's feet. "How much you gettin' for them radios?"

He hesitated before answering, "Twenty a piece."

"An' you got 'bout what... five or six of 'em?" He nodded. "So, you tellin' me, for a hunid dollars, you willin' to do fifteen-to-life?"

Juan-Juan looked at him sideways.

"Well, that's exactly what them honkies woulda gave you if you woulda got caught. Here it is you just kilt a man, and you worried about some muthafuckin' stolen radios. 'Bout to hand yo' life over to them people for some shit that ain't even gon' last you two months in prison. Let me ask you somethin', Youngblood. Do you know the difference between knowledge and wisdom?"

Juan-Juan thought for a second, then slowly shook his head.

"Knowledge is knowing. Wisdom is applying. You gotta apply what you know. Just because a man is knowledgeable don't mean he wise. His moves... his actions… his way of life. Those are the things that will determine whether or not he has wisdom."

Juan-Juan was all ears as the old-head continued to lace him. "Learn to get in tune wit' and follow yo' instincts. I don't care what it is you doin' or how much money involved, if somethin' don't feel right or shit ain't goin' according to plan, haul ass. Don't let greed be yo' downfall. 'Cause it only takes a split-second to be in handcuffs, and I've seen it take niggas years to get them bitches off. Take heed, Youngblood. Some shit you don't gotta learn through experience."

Later that night, he walked Juan-Juan halfway home and told him he would see him around. "An' remember, freedom is priceless. You don't toy wit' no shit like that."

Juan-Juan nodded; the look in his eyes allowing Terry Jones to see that the murder he had just committed would be the first of many.

* * *

Leaning down with his hands on his knees, Terry Jones looked in through the passenger side window and smiled. "Hey, Youngblood, when you get out?"

"This mornin'."

Terry nodded, pleased by the answer.

Juan-Juan waved his hand in invitation. "Hop in."

Terry's smile suddenly faded as he looked away. "Naw, not right now, Youngblood," he said quietly.

Juan-Juan frowned in confusion. Not right now? Then it suddenly dawned on him. His clothes. He didn't want to sit his dirty-clothed body on the white seats. Juan-Juan leaned over and opened the passenger door. "Fuck this car."

He took him to get something to eat, bought him a bottle, then put some change in his pockets. Terry tried to refuse it at first, but Juan-Juan wasn't budging. He thought back to the day when he had logged onto the prison's computer and saw that $6.00 had been wired into his account. He smirked when he saw the sender's last name was Jones. Every

Kweli

month that followed, until his release, Terry would send him no less than $5.00.

Juan-Juan knew niggas in prison who didn't get nothing from their men in the streets. Men who were in the mix. But here was a homeless man who was able to scrounge up money every month for someone he considered a friend. The amount was small, but the gesture was monumental. Terry Jones had once said that a man will define himself, not by his words, but according to his actions.

As part of their ritual, Juan-Juan parked back in front of the abandoned house and listened as Terry dropped jewels. "See, Youngblood, a lot of niggas fall short out here 'cause they don't know the difference between seeing an' observing. Niggas gettin' robbed, killed, doin' football numbers in prison, and can't reach certain levels in the game, all because they don't know the difference between seeing and observing." He took a swig and continued, "I 'member I was in the joint some years back, and I used to see niggas playin' chess all day long, and I wondered how many of them knew the difference between seeing and observing. So, I waited till they wasn't around no chess boards, then I asked some of em' the same question, 'How many squares on a chess board?'" He looked at Juan-Juan in disbelief. "Do you know that only a few of them niggas gave the right answer? We talkin' 'bout some people who stare at a board for hours a day, everyday. But didn't know how many squares it had on it. That's because they was seeing... but not observing.

64

The Cost of Loyalty

"We miss a lot in life like that, Youngblood. And being as though we only get one shot at this shit, missin' out is somethin' we really can't afford to do. You gotta be alert at all times. Watching. Studying. Observing. And that's what separates the good from the great... the alive from the dead."

Terry Jones' spiel continued to echo in Juan-Juan's ears as he drove back out to Springfield Township later that day.

Kweli

CHAPTER 7

JBo and Olivia were in the Hellcat feeling themselves off that T.I. and Marsha Ambrosius song, "Dope". She was snapping her fingers and dancing in her seat while he rapped along with T.I. and dangerously swerved in and out of lanes.

"You don't talk much, do you?" Tonya asked Juan-Juan as they trailed JBo and Olivia to Glass City. In her seat at an angle, she was watching him as he handled the big-body with ease; even managing to keep up with the Hellcat.

"Why, wassup?" He replied without taking his eyes off the road.

"Naw, it's just, you know. I hope you not uncomfortable by that lil' situation. 'Cause, like I said earlier, that wasn't my first encounter wit' somethin' like that. So, trust me, you ain't got nothin' to worry 'bout."

Her words falling on deaf ears, he nodded.

Arriving at the club, they drew envious stares and mumbled curses as JBo marched them to the front of the line. And it didn't help that both men—who wore linen short-sets and Mauri gator sandals—had trophies on their arms. Her seductive eyes peering from behind over-sized Gucci shades, Olivia was rocking a fitted sweater-dress with suede ankle boots, while Tonya was looking scandalous in an all red Phillip Lim jumpsuit with no panties; her obese pussy-lips on full display.

After slipping the bouncer a nickel to go in without being wanded down, they were admitted into the expensively furnished building where the crowd was turned up off Rick Ross' "Rich Forever".

Acknowledgements and head-nods were plentiful as they were being escorted to their booth in VIP. Just as a barely-dressed waitress approached their table for drink orders, a heavy-weight named Kool-Aid and two of his renegades-in-training were led into the room and seated at a nearby table. As he scanned his surroundings, it was only a matter of time before he saw Juan-Juan and JBo. A glutton for attention, he animatedly threw his arms up.

They looked him off.

When he foolishly got up and came over to their table, JBo knew the night was already on the verge of turning sour.

"When you niggas get out?" A jeweled-up Kool-Aid smiled as he draped his arm around the waitress. Despite his strong resemblance to the late rapper Biggie Smalls, the amount of money he generated from heroin sales allowed him to feel at ease when in the presence of bad bitches. He understood the advantages that came along with having a bag.

"Scram, nigga," Juan-Juan said through gritted teeth; his cold stare forcing Kool-Aid to avert his eyes.

"Damn, baby." He turned to JBo with a goofy expression. "It's like that?"

"We hip to you, bra." He shrugged nonchalantly. "So just fall back."

The three men had been at the detention center in Milan, Michigan, when Kool-Aid allegedly left for sentencing and never came back. Their suspicion aroused, JBo had Olivia got on Pacer and looked him up. She sent an email back the next day, reading, "He out." They later found out Kool-Aid was the type of rodent they both despised. A rat.

Before Kool-Aid could respond, Juan-Juan stood up from the table. "Get the fuck on."

The waitress peeled his arm from around her neck and scurried off as the two young renegades, Boo-Boo and Smurf, rushed over. "Wassup, 'Laid?" Boo-Boo asked as he tried to hold Juan-Juan's stare. "You straight?"

When JBo jumped up, Olivia quickly followed suit. "Can y'all please just go back to your table?" she politely asked Kool-Aid. "We just got here, and would just like to enjoy our night."

Boo-Boo waved her off. "Sit yo' black-ass down somewhere, bitch!"

Olivia grabbed JBo as he lunged forward. "Baby, no!"

Noticing the commotion, two John Cena-built security guards made their way over. "Is there a problem over here?"

"Naw, ain't no problem," Juan-Juan quickly spoke up. "We don't want no trouble," he added, placing both hands in the air as a sign of retreat, which was strictly for the cameras. He then turned to JBo and nudged his head toward the door. "Let's get up outta here."

Outside, in the parking lot, Juan-Juan pulled JBo aside. "Let Tonya ride back with you and Olivia."

"Let that shit go, my nigga! We can go somewhere else," JBo responded.

Juan-Juan shook his head in disagreement.

"Well, I'm comin' wit' you then."

Again, he shook his head. "Just go on and dip," he said, taking his strap off his waist and handing it to JBo. "This light work."

When Juan-Juan left the club, he drove around the corner and parked at the end of a block. Grabbing a duffel bag out of the trunk, he was in all black within minutes. He reached under his seat and pulled out a stainless steel .40, click-clacked one in the head, then pulled the slide back just enough to ensure that a Hydro-Shock was in place.

With the strap in the small of his back, he hid his car keys behind the wheel closest to the curb, then pulled his hood on and marched back around to the club.

* * *

"Man, them niggas Juan-Juan and JBo ain't built like that for real, Blood," Boo-Boo slurred, feeling extra courageous off the liquor. "They in this bitch in sandals and shit. Them niggas hoes!"

"I feel you, Gotti," Smurf chimed in. "'Cause on my momma, I started to take flight on one of them bitch-ass niggas."

As they continued barking, Kool-Aid couldn't shake the nervous feeling he had in the pit of his stomach. In all the time he had known Juan-Juan and JBo, them backing down was unheard of. Juan-Juan was known for embracing confrontation. *Maybe the joint done softened 'em up*, he tried to reason with himself as he downed the rest of his drink.

When closing time came around, Kool-Aid followed his intuition and handed his keys to Boo-

Boo. "Y'all go start the car up, and I'ma take a piss real quick."

He might've been a rat, but, when necessary, he knew how to be cautious as a serpent.

* * *

Under the cloak of darkness, Juan-Juan was anxiously crouched beside a large dumpster when people began to emerge from the club. He frowned behind the mask as he saw Boo-Boo and Smurf exit the club without Kool-Aid. *Nigga in there hidin'*, he fumed to himself.

Smurf was first to see the faceless gunman coming toward them in all black. He froze in his tracks while Boo-Boo tried to cut out.

BOC! BOC!

Two leg-shots sent him face-first onto the pavement. In a fluid motion, Juan-Juan swung the gun around and hit Smurf in the stomach.

BOC!

Pandemonium instantly ignited throughout the parking lot.

As Boo-Boo tried to crawl toward the club's entrance, Juan-Juan ceased his movements with a vicious rib-kick that made him throw up. He then grabbed him by the collar and drug him next to Smurf, who was holding his stomach in an attempt to keep his intestines from falling out.

Juan-Juan lifted his mask and watched in satisfaction as their eyes widened in surprise.

"Come on, Gotti, it wasn't even like that," Smurf cried. "We was just tryna impress Kool-Aid."

"See you when I get there," he farewelled before he bit his bottom lip and forcefully fired three in his face.

BOC! BOC! BOC!

"Fuck you, nigga!" Boo-Boo spat, refusing to go like a coward.

"Likewise," Juan-Juan replied before he pleasurably ensured him a closed casket. To him, there was nothing like standing up over a nigga and, while staring him in his eyes, dumping several rounds into his head.

Purposely leaving the gun at the crime scene, he jogged to a nearby alley to set his work clothes on fire, then calmly walked back to the 'Lac and pulled off, listening to Plies' "Murkin' Season".

"The wrong place to play games, boy the streets real... tryna impress a muthafucka what get you niggas killed... Murkin' season is official, boy this shit for real!"

CHAPTER 8

JBo was standing outside the condo, worriedly smoking a Mild when Juan-Juan finally pulled up; his eyes still dancing with excitement.

"Wassup? You straight?" JBo asked in relief as they slapped hands.

"I couldn't get Kool-Aid," he answered in disappointment.

Flicking the Mild, JBo took a deep breath as he put his head down and pinched the bridge of his nose. "My nigga, I thought the whole point in us turnin' down the halfway house was so that we could get out and get straight to it?"

Juan-Juan nodded.

"But how we gon' do that if we out here goin' to war wit' niggas? That shit ain't gon' put food in our stomachs."

Juan-Juan looked off.

"Listen to me, fam," JBo continued with a solemn expression. "I luh you to death, but I'm tryna hit this sting and get the fuck on, and I'm hopin' you on the same page. 'Cause we both know what our options is if we stay stuck in this small ass city, doin' the same shit. We gotta give ourselves a chance, my nigga. Don't we deserve that?"

He slowly nodded.

"Well, let's stay under the radar for a minute and get back on track."

As soon as they entered the condo, Tonya got off the couch and ran to Juan-Juan. "You feel better now? JBo told us how you like to drive on the expressway when you upset."

"Yeah, I'm good," he replied, silently thanking JBo for thinking ahead.

"Gimme a hug," Tonya said, pulling him into an embrace. With her arms around his neck, she whispered in his ear, "I want you to come home wit' me tonight."

* * *

Before the police could arrive at Glass City, Kool-Aid had slipped out the club's backdoor and crept around to the parking lot. He spotted his keys lying near Boo-Boo's lifeless body. Hurriedly snatching them up, he jumped in his 760 and peeled out.

While keeping a watchful eye on his mirrors, he phoned his most ruthless and experienced shooter, D-Wub. "Round the troops up and meet me on Page, Gotti."

The apartment was crowded with foot soldiers who thrived on chaos when Kool-Aid stepped inside. Their hobby was popping Mollies and dropping bodies, then forgetting about it by the next day.

Kool-Aid gave an edited version of what happened at the club, leaving out the part where he knowingly sent Boo-Boo and Smurf outside to their demise. Feigning grief behind their deaths, he turned to D-Wub with a saddened expression. "Stop by they momma house tomorrow and drop off fifteen racks, and let her know I send my condolences."

Light-skinned with heavy ink and a good grade of hair, stylishy-cut into a mohawk, D-Wub was seated on a couch, taking measured pulls from a stick of Bubba while caressing the head of his most loyal and trusted friend, Bella— an all-black fierce-looking Pitbull with a Red Boy and Jeep bloodline. He had purchased her from the Mountain Man when she was a puppy. By her first birthday, he had transformed her into a Land Shark.

D-Wub's crib had once been the random target of a B and E. After loudly knocking on the front door to ensure that no one was home, the burglar jimmied open a downstairs window and started to crawl head-first into the darkened house. He was halfway inside when his instincts made him look up. He found himself staring into the deadliest pair of eyes he had ever seen. His bladder released just before Bella locked her powerful jaws around his throat and crushed his windpipe. When D-Wub returned home two hours later, Bella was still lying on the floor, locked on to his throat; waiting for permission to release.

Only D-Wub's inner circle knew that while she was still a puppy, he had found a veterinarian to surgically remove her vocal cords. So, unless you were right there in her face when she barked, the noise that came from her was soundless. A shark on land.

"Startin' tomorrow," Kool-Aid heatedly continued. "I want niggas on twenty-four-hour manhunts. I got twenty-five racks for each head. And if you get 'em both at the same time, that's an extra dub."

Unbeknownst to anyone on Kool-Aid's team, his hunger for vengeance went beyond the deaths of Boo-Boo and Smurf. Casualties were a part of life, and it wasn't that he was afraid of Juan-Juan and JBo exposing him as being a rat, because he knew that when you're making it possible for men to live luxurious lifestyles, majority of them will disregard the rules that once governed the streets. Principles were becoming extinct. But this was on a more personal level. A resentment he had been harboring toward both men for many years now. For the attempt on his life— which was the final straw— he was now willing to pay whatever fee necessary to ensure that they slept in pine boxes before the month was out.

Kool-Aid was punching the Beamer out to his five-bedroom in Ottawa Hills when he got a two-worded text from a young bust-down he had been chasing for a week. "You up?"

He bypassed the small talk and called her. "What you say I come through and let you bounce on this mu'fucka till the mall open up? Then we can go cop that new Louie bag you saw the other day."

His proposal made her respond accordingly. "Hurry up, Darius. Wit' yo' nasty self."

* * *

"Juan-Juan, slow down!" Tonya screamed as he mercilessly punished her with jackhammer-like strokes.

With one knee dug into the couch and his other leg on the floor for support, he had her balled up with her head mashed into a corner of the couch. When he continued to crush her as if he had no intentions of slowing down, she angled her head to where she could see his face. As if in a trance, he was staring through her.

"Juan-Juan, stop!" She yelled, pinching his thigh hard enough to make him flinch.

His eyes blinked several times before snapping back to reality.

"Let my legs down, baby," she said gently.

Avoiding eye contact as he stepped into his briefs, he asked her where the bathroom was.

"Down the hall, to the left." She pointed while staring at his back with a puzzled expression. She reached out to touch it and he quickly slapped her hand away, and froze her with a piercing stare.

When he came back into the living room and started getting dressed, Tonya unleashed her curiosity. "What happened to yo' back?" She asked in regards to the small grayish bumps that were scattered across it.

"Why? Wassup?" He countered sharply.

"Everybody not the enemy, Juan-Juan," she replied in a sincere tone. "I can tell you've been through a lot, and how will you ever get rid of the pain if you never let it out?"

Through the eyes of vicious but severely wounded animal, he just glared at her before continuing to get dressed. Even if he wanted to, how could he tell her that the scars on his back were from his foster parents burning him with lit cigarettes when he was only eight years old? Despite his screams, they would hold him down and take turns using his back as an ashtray.

As Tonya was lying in bed that night, she couldn't help but wonder what had been going through Juan-Juan's mind when they were having sex. She would have found it quite disturbing if she knew that he had actually been replaying the double homicide he had just put down hours earlier.

CHAPTER 9

"Let em' see that monsta in me. Load MG-thirty, leave the crib and bring that choppa wit' me." While banging Meek Mill's "The Plug" at a high volume, Juan-Juan and JBo were floating down I-75 in a stolen Monte Carlo. From head-to-toe they were draped in all black and wore Kevlar vests beneath their hoodies. On their way to the D—Detroit—both men were in a zone as they mentally readied themselves for the mayhem they were about to inflict.

After doing their homework, they learned it would take nearly 50-racks to hit the lick from Juan-Juan's dream. And they were short by forty. Without the patience or desire to grind it out, they turned to what they did best— laying niggas down.

Because they carefully camouflaged themselves as legitimate hustlers, no one in the city even suspected them as being responsible for a string of deadly robberies over the years. It was after their second lick when JBo's wisdom came into play. "We can't let niggas get hip to us, bra," he counseled Juan-Juan one night as they counted out $29,000 and weighed 17-ounces of Hard. "'Cause niggas that's out here chewin' gon' be on alert if they know what we on, and we tryna leave 'em sleep. So, instead of dumpin' this work off, we gon' bust these bitches down and start trappin'. Fuck being known as jack-boys, we gon' be known for hustlin', and watch as doors start to open."

His vision soon proved to be on point, as victims became plentiful. They left bullet-riddled bodies all over the city. Some were found tortured in their ransacked homes, while others were stuffed in the trunks of their cars with terrified expressions frozen on their faces.

Arriving in the D forty-minutes later, JBo drove to the eastside, where they were about to pay a terminal visit to a nigga called Pinewood-T.

JBo had gotten hip to him through Ciara, a female he used to occasionally knock down before going to the feds. Thick as gumbo with a light-skinned complexion and a Dej Loaf hair-style, she had a master's degree in Headology that would often summon him to her doorstep in the middle of the night.

Ciara saw him in traffic a few days after his release and flagged him down. Knowing he just came home, she wanted some dick that only a nigga fresh out could provide.

JBo shot her down. On the strength that Olivia had just rode shotgun for two-years, he couldn't see himself doing her dirty in less than a week after getting out.

Not easily deterred, Ciara lured him in with a business proposal. "I know you been gone a minute, and them pockets pro'ly gotta slow leak." She looked down and hungrily eyed his dick print before reaching out and squeezing it. "You gimme a shot of this, and I'll turn you on to a sweet-ass lick up in the D."

Knowing her sexual exploits enabled her to mingle with the elite, JBo was in the Budget-Inn thirty minutes later, blowing her back out. He made her scream everything she knew about Pinewood-T as he dogged her all over the room.

Before parting ways, Ciara assured him that it would be an easy and worthwhile lick. "The fat nigga got a bag, so make sho' you bless me after you handle yo' business." In gray leggings and no panties, he watched her ass cheeks clap as she nastily strutted toward her hot-pink Charger.

When JBo bent a left onto Pinewood-T's street, he and Juan-Juan frowned as they noticed a small crowd gathered in the field next to the green house. As if some type of party was underway, Patron bottles and Kush blunts were in rotation while half-naked females gyrated to music that boomed from one of the cars parked in the field. This was a scenario neither man had anticipated.

Circling the block, JBo parked down the street from the house and killed the engine. It was now a matter of patience.

An hour later, as they sat low in the Monte, a '69 Cutty on 30-inch Dub Rolex's sped past. Candy orange with black rally stripes and dual pipes, the oldie loudly braked in front of the green house, then drove up on the curb and parked in the front yard. A chubby dark-skinned nigga with dreads and a well-groomed beard hopped out with a chrome Desert in hand. He knew he was a jack-boy's target and kept a high-caliber pistol within arm's reach at all times.

"That's the nigga right there," JBo quietly announced, recognizing him from a picture on Ciara's phone.

Anxious for action, Juan-Juan reached into the backseat and lifted up a blue blanket. He grabbed a

FNH with two ladders taped together, and passed it to JBo. And for himself, he picked up a Chopper with the Monkey-Nuts. "You go in through the back and get that nigga, and I'ma handle this lil' shit out front." He saw the questioning look in JBo's eyes and assured him, "I got this, my nigga." He click-clacked one in the head. "Now, go get what we came fo' while I fill up a morgue."

As he watched JBo creep between two houses, Juan-Juan put in ear-plugs before pulling the Jason mask down over his face. Then, like a Roman gladiator, he fearlessly stepped out of the car and onto the battlefield.

Crouching beside the Monte, he duck-walked down the street until he was positioned directly across from the crowd. With no regard for human life, he rose up from on the passenger side of a Ford Fusion and leaned over the roof.

TAT! TAT! TAT! TAT! TAT! TAT! TAT! TAT! TAT! TAT! TAT! TAT!

In one sweep, the finger-size slugs from the assault rifle chopped down five men and one unfortunate woman.

As the surviving women screamed in terror and mindlessly scattered, a few niggas followed suit, while two others scrambled behind a foreign and returned fire.

BOK! BOK! BOK! BOK! BOK! BOK! BOK!

Juan-Juan ducked behind the car just as shattered glass rained down over him. Grinning psychotically, he began to wildly bob his head to the music that continued to play from across the street.

* * *

JBo was crouched at the back of the house when he heard the exchange of gunfire. He immediately stood up and booted the back door in. With the FNH correctly held in both hands, he crept into the house, waving it from side-to-side, prepared to squeeze at the slightest movement.

BOOM! BOOM! BOOM! BOOM!

JBo dove next to the refrigerator as someone discharged what sounded like a cannon into the kitchen. His heart instantly started pounding. *I can't get hit by no shit like that,* he nervously thought as he fixed his ski-mask. After forcing himself into a state of calmness, he was able to come up with a strategy.

Knowing from experience that most powerful handguns usually held no more than ten rounds, he stuck his arm out and blindly fired a barrage of shots into the front room.

His opponent responded just as he had expected.

BOOM! BOOM! BOOM! BOOM!

When JBo heard the gun being reloaded, he raced into the front room with the FNH leading the way.

* * *

Playtime over, Juan-Juan rose from behind the bullet-riddled Fusion and boldly advanced toward his adversaries.

TAT! TAT! TAT! TAT! TAT! TAT! TAT! TAT! TAT! TAT! TAT! TAT!

Holding the chopper up high, he loved the way it bucked in his arms while the spent shell-casings made musical sounds as they clink-clink-clinked onto the pavement.

As he closed in on the car the two shooters hid behind, he deliberately eased up off the trigger. They took the bait and came up to return fire.

TAT! TAT! TAT! TAT! TAT! TAT! TAT! TAT!

Their deaths were instant, but honorable; as their last breath was taken while still clutching their firearms.

As Juan-Juan heartlessly swaggered pass the fallen soldiers, he smirked to himself as a rap by the Ghetto-Boys suddenly popped in his head.

"You cried when yo' grandmother died, and that was real... but you ain't gotta cry no mo; you goin' to see her."

* * *

When JBo saw Pinewood-T standing beside an empty fish tank slapping in another clip, he aimed low and squeezed.

BOK! BOK! BOK!

"Aaarrgghh!" He cried out, the Desert Eagle slipping from his hand as he collapsed to the floor.

"I'm leaving here wit' one of two thangs," JBo said as he kicked the gun across the room. "Yo' life, or yo' money. Now, which is it?"

"Look in the 'frigerator," Pinewood-T groaned as he held his thigh and rocked back and forth in agony. "In the beer cans. Unscrew 'em from the bottom."

"Move and I'm squeezing," JBo warned as backed toward the kitchen. He heard a noise from behind and swung his gun around.

Juan-Juan stepped inside the kitchen, eyes wild with excitement.

Using the distraction to his advantage, Pinewood-T was up and running.

JBo spun around and let off four shots as he dove head-first through the front window. Juan-Juan was about to give chase, but JBo grabbed his arm. "Fuck 'im."

He quickly snatched open the refrigerator, grabbed one of the beer cans and shook it, then pulled a trash bag from inside his pants leg and raked the cans into it. As he turned to leave, his eyes instinctively went to the top of the refrigerator, where he remembered seeing Coffee and Pringle cans when he first entered the house. Taking no chances, he grabbed them all.

With the bag slung over his shoulder, he and Juan-Juan fled out the backdoor, leaving behind nearly 200 spent shell-casings and the stench of death from an eight-body massacre.

Kweli

CHAPTER 10

After torching the Monte behind a vacant building, JBo hit Fat-Cat on the jack and said two words— "B.B. King."

It took Fat-Cat only a split second to pick up on the lingo. The Blues. "Meet me at the McDonalds out on Secor."

When JBo was punching the Monte Carlo back from the D, he had told Juan-Juan to go through all the cans. The suspense was killing him. Inside the Redbull and Budweiser's— which unscrewed from the top— were sandwich bags full of Roxy's. There were thousands of the small blue pills. When he unscrewed one of the coffee cans from the bottom and rubber-banded rolls of money tumbled out, JBo looked over and yelled, "Nigga, we rich!"

Five minutes after Juan-Juan and JBo pulled into the McDonalds' parking lot, Fat-Cat drove up in a raggedy-ass Ford Tempo. In a Ralph Lauren hooded sweat suit and the latest LeBron's, he jumped in the Lac's backseat.

"I see you keepin' a low profile." JBo smiled as they slapped hands.

"Be discreet and leave 'em sleep, you feel me?" He then tapped the back of Juan-Juan's seat. "What's good, bra?"

Slouched down with his hood on and a 500-Revolver within arm's reach, he responded in a dry tone, "Shit." He would never fall asleep on a man he had once assaulted; no matter how long ago.

Breaking the tension, JBo tossed Fat-Cat all five cans. "Unscrew 'em from the top."

With all ten bags laid out on the seat, he eyed them closely before looking up. "Let me check one out real quick."

JBo shrugged. "Do yo' thang."

He pulled up Google on his Galaxy, then compared a random pill from the bag to one on the screen. "It's about four thousand of these bitches," he said as he placed the pill back inside the bag. "I can send 'em down to West-V for like twenty-five a-pop. So, I'm sayin', shid, I'll give you seventy-five racks for all of 'em right now."

Doing no faking, JBo agreed without hesitation. "Bet."

Fat-Cat tapped the screen and put the phone to his ear. "Bring me seventy-five on the grown side." His phone rung ten minutes later as a green Infinity truck steered into the parking lot. "Pull on the driver side of the 'Lac, straight in front of you."

This nigga on some real boss shit, JBo admitted to himself with a subtle nod. Wordlessly, and without much eye contact, a Selena Gomez look-a-like handled the exchange; pulling off before her tinted window was completely raised.

* * *

At JBo's Apartment

After slowly and carefully hand-counting the money several times, Juan-Juan and JBo stared in amazement at what was lying on the dinning room table. $147,356. Being in the presence of so much money gave JBo a euphoric feeling that made him break out in goose bumps. The moment felt unreal.

Juan-Juan glanced at him, easily recognizing a familiar look in his eyes. "Wassup, my nigga?"

JBo smiled, knowing they were in each other's minds.

Juan-Juan just smirked.

"Listen to me, bra," He said, clapping his hands together excitedly. "After we get everything we need for this move, I gotta mean-ass idea. I'm talkin' 'bout we gon' fuck the whole city wit' this. Watch."

After hiding the money in various parts of the apartment, they had to literally force themselves to lay down and get some sleep. Tomorrow would be a busy day, requiring full tanks of energy and alert minds.

* * *

FCI Manchester

When the cell doors were popped for breakfast at 6AM, T-Woods and Ham were two of the first inmates to emerge from their rooms. Suited up in workout gear— a prison issued toboggan, tattered gray sweats, and black steel toes— they met up at one of the microwaves.

"I hollered at that nigga Juan-Juan last night," T-Woods quietly informed as he placed a strong cup of straight-black into the microwave. "He say be ready to hit the ground runnin' soon as we touch down." Towering at 6'4" and a solid 235 pounds, T-Woods was dark-skinned with a bald head and a chipped front tooth that resulted from his gladiator days in juvie. He had the type of heart that would not allow him to back down from no one; which was evident by the permanently bruised knuckles on his over-sized mitts.

"That's cool," Ham said with a deep scowl, "but I still ain't feelin' how them niggas tryna carry us. They got us signing up for some shit, and we don't even know what the fuck it is." Rocking a Boosie fade over a caramel complexion, Ham suffered from a small-man complex. He had a hair-trigger temper and would heatedly debate over the simplest things.

"I feel you," T-Woods agreed as he removed the cup from the microwave. "But sometimes you gotta put yo' emotions aside so you can see the bigger picture." He then chugged his half and handed the cup to Ham. This was part of their pre-workout ritual that was designed to boost their energy levels.

"What's the bigger picture?" Ham questioned right before he turned the cup up and downed the rest of the motor oil.

T-Woods flashed a devious grin while stroking his James Harden-like beard. "Four people can keep a secret if two of 'em dead."

Ham chuckled as he gave him dap. "That's law."

Hailing from the west side of Cleveland, Ohio, both men were project babies who knew only one way. Like so many countless others throughout the nation, poverty and neglect had driven them toward illicit lifestyles. Their criminal careers consisted of B and E's, selling small quantities of work, and committing botched robberies. They hungered for more, but there had never been any opportunities. So now that they were being invited to partake in a million dollar feast, they would take full advantage.

The Cost of Loyalty

When T-Woods and Ham entered the recreation building, both men calmly walked through the metal detectors as if a 6-inch 'Floater'—a fiber glass knife—wasn't attached to the drawstrings on the insides of their shorts. Because violence could ignite anywhere at any given moment, one had to always be prepared and ready.

They would start their workout off with 500 push-ups, then go inside the weight-pile and hit ten sets of 225 on the flat-bench. As T-Woods was on the ground, effortlessly knocking out his set of 'ups, he was unable to see Ham standing over with a facial expression that mirrored his inner-thought. *Shid, fuck what this nigga talkin' 'bout. Only way four people can keep a secret is if three of 'em dead.*

Kweli

CHAPTER 11

Following a trip to the DMV—where they paid the $180.00 reinstatement fee for Juan-Juan's license—they caught a cab to a used car lot and bought two cars reliable enough to put on the road. In a Crown Vic, JBo would shoot to Columbus to fill in certain blanks concerning the lick, while Juan-Juan would drive to Pennsylvania and switch cars with a man named Bobby-Ray. For 25-racks, the most important thing needed for the lick would be hidden inside of a white Hyundai.

JBo's old cellie— who had served in the military before being dishonorably discharged— had orchestrated the deal only after JBo agreed to wire him $2,000 the day it went through. "Call it a mediator's fee," he had said with a smile. Doing a 20-year sentence for selling guns on the black market, JBo didn't have a problem looking out for a man who had took his own weight.

After stopping at a public library and using their internet to go online and make a $3,500 purchase, JBo was on his way back to the car when he got a call from a number he didn't recognize. "Hello?"

"So, that's how you gon' play yo' hand, huh?" Ciara asked.

"Fuck is you talkin' 'bout?"

"Nigga, don't try to play dumb. I know you hit that lick!"

"Where you at?" he asked, scanning the parking lot.

"Naw, nigga, the question is, where the fuck is my cut at?"

JBo struggled for self-control. "Aye, listen, I'ma get back wit' you later on, 'cause you talkin' real reckless right now."

"You know what? Don't even worry 'bout it, 'cause I ain't scared of you or that nigga Ju—"

He hung up before she could finish. *Damn, I hope I'on gotta do nothin' to this bitch*, he thought as he slid behind the wheel of the Crown Vic. Making a mental note to check her temperature as soon as he got back to the city, he eased out of the parking lot and merged in with traffic.

* * *

D-Wub walked into a well-known beauty salon called Platinum's, drug a chair in the middle of the room, then stood up on it. "Aye, I need everybody to shut the fuck and listen!" Since the night of Boo-Boo and Smurf's death, his manhunt had been relentless.

"Girl, who this nigga thank he is?" One woman loudly whispered to the woman seated next to her.

"I'on know. But bitch, the nigga is fine."

D-Wub silenced both women with a stare that made them quickly glance toward the floor.

"Now, like I was sayin'. I'm lookin' I for them niggas Juan-Juan and JBo, an' I got twenty racks for whoever can point me in the right direction."

Chatter instantly erupted throughout the shop at the mention of so much money.

He yelled for everyone to quiet down. "I'ma give y'all a number to reach me at. But I'm warning you now, don't waste my time wit' no dumb shit." He then drug out a stack of blue faces and passed one out to each person in the room. "My number wrote on the bills. I'on give a fuck what time of the day it is, if you know somethin' or can find it out, the money is yours."

For additional proof that money was not an issue, he asked who the owner of the shop was. When a shapely-built woman named Patrice spoke up, he told her to meet him at the register, "Everything on me!"

The women went ham.

While at the counter counting out $4,200, Patrice tried to shoot her shot at the younger man. "I can take an early lunch break if you wanna go grab something to eat."

"I'm here on business, ma," he politely declined. "Maybe another time."

D-Wub was on his way back to his Ford Raptor when he noticed Bella watching him through the driver's side window with an intense stare. Without breaking stride, he smoothly withdrew a P-89 from under his Polo jacket and spun around. "Fuck is you creepin' up behind me fo'?" He gritted as the Ruger's mouth kissed the forehead of an attractive female.

Paralyzed with fear, she was unable to speak.

Recognizing the look of genuine terror in her eyes, he instinctively decided that she posed no threat. "You can't be doin' shit like that," he scolded her as he tucked the hammer back on his waist.

Placing a hand over her chest, she playfully pushed him. "Boy, you almost gave me a heart attack."

"Naw, bitch, you lucky I ain't give you a head-shot." Unaffected by her looks, he glanced at his watch impatiently. "So, what's on yo' mind?"

Guiding him toward the Raptor, she looked back at the shop for prying eyes before saying in a hushed tone, "I know Juan-Juan and JBo."

CHAPTER 12

When JBo got back from Columbus later that day, he had one last stop to make at an auto body shop on the east side, called Rocky's. It was rumored that because most of his clientele was street-oriented, he accepted payments of cash, jewelry, or drugs— whichever was more convenient. And for that reason, he had been JBo's first selection.

Wheeling into the parking lot, he noticed a pint-size man standing out front, sucking on a cancer-stick. He wore a tired expression along with a tan Dickie suit, speckled with paint.

"'Scuse me," JBo said as he approached the egg-shaped man. "You know if Rocky around?"

He exhaled a cloud of toxic fumes toward the sky before answering in a raspy voice, "Ya' lookin' at 'im."

JBo smirked at the fact that he was nothing like what he had imagined. "I'm tryna get some work done on two cars."

"Shouldn't be a problem."

"But only under two conditions."

A head nod signaled for JBo to continue.

"One is that the work be done by you, and you alone. The second is that you agree to take this with you to yo' grave. If you can't agree to both terms, then I'll get back in my car and drive off, and we never met."

Rocky took a long pull off the cigarette, then dropped it on the ground and stubbed it out with the tip of his boot. "You a cop?" He questioned as he stared up into JBo's eyes, and smoke rings curling from his nostrils.

He shook his head.

"So, let's say I were to agree. Exactly how would you be paying?"

Letting the money talk, JBo drug a bankroll out of his cargo pants.

Revealing tobacco-stained teeth, the little man beamed, "Let's go in my office."

When JBo finished explaining what he needed done, Rocky was no longer smiling. In fact, he had a strong urge to push the $5,000 down-payment back across his desk and tell JBo to get lost. But his instincts warned him that there would be repercussions if he decided to back out at this point.

After reaching an agreement on the full price and a deadline date, they sealed the deal with a handshake, then Rocky rushed him out of his office; saying he had more work to do.

As he stood outside hot-boxing a cancer-stick, his eyes followed the Crown Vic's taillights until they were no longer visible. "What the fuck have I gotten myself into?" he mumbled to himself before flicking the cigarette and turning to go back inside.

* * *

"Shorty sittin' low; big thangs poppin'... Tip on a glock from a Crip up in Compton."

Juan-Juan was doing the speed limit back to Ohio when his phone started vibrating on his lap. Seeing JBo's name on the screen, he paused the music and answered. "What up, bra?"

"What's good, my nigga? You straight?"

"Aint no mystery."

"A'ight, that's wassup. Well, look. I'm 'bout to go take care of my old cellie real quick, then I'ma shoot over to Olivia's. So, just hit me up when you close to the crib, and I'll meet you there."

"A'ight."

"A'ight, my nigga."

"To another chapter, paper that I capture. Caught up in the rapture of gunshots and laughter. Homicide is humor and nigga you lookin' funny..." Rick Ross' Mafia Music.

* * *

On the phone with Tonya, Olivia was lying in bed nursing a drink when she heard JBo enter the condo. Hurriedly getting off the phone, she put her drink on the nightstand and raced downstairs.

"Hi, baby!" Olivia cheesed as she threw her arms around JBo's neck and pulled him into an affectionate-starved kiss.

"Damn, girl," he moaned as she trailed sensual kisses from his face to his neck.

"I've been missing you, baby," she crooned into his ear. "I haven't seen you in three days." When he volunteered no explanation, she looked up at him with a concerned expression. "What's going on with you?"

He shook his head. "It ain't shit. I just gotta handle a few things wit' Juan- Juan." He planted a kiss on her forehead. "So, I Just need you to sit tight for a minute."

Staring in his eyes, Olivia asked, "Do you believe in your heart that I love you unconditionally?"

After hardly a moment's thought, he nodded.

"Do you consider me your partner in life? One that will never abandon you, regardless of the circumstances?"

Again, he nodded.

"Well, there shouldn't be nothing we can't discuss. Because how can we really call ourselves a team if we have secrets between us? I know I'm not from the streets, so my knowledge might be limited in that area. But because I accept you for who you are, I should at least be given the chance to try and understand certain aspects of your life." She placed her hand on the side of his face and gently caressed it. "I love you with all my heart. Therefore, I believe that gives me the right to know what's going on with my man. I've proven myself to you, Javonte. So, you have absolutely no reason not to trust me."

When he stood there and just looked at her, she turned to walk away. He grabbed her arm. "Where you goin', baby?"

"Don't you baby me!" She spazzed with tearful eyes. "I have been nothing but good to you from day one. I carried myself like a true lady while you were in that place. Gave you the loyalty that men in there dream of, but rarely receive. But yet you have the audacity to stand here and act like you gotta keep something from me?" She began to slowly shake her head. "I don't know if I can do this anymore. Maybe our relationship isn't what I thought it was."

Her threat caused his heart to instantly sink to his stomach; exposing just how much he had become mentally dependent upon her. If she were to leave, it would uncover the emotional void in him that she had managed to fill. So, him being unable to digest the thought of her leaving, he began to foolishly reason with himself. *She has been in the whip since day one. Only a thorough bitch capable of stayin' on her pivot while a nigga do a bid, and I know she wouldn't do nothin' to jeopardize my freedom.*

Pulling her back into his arms, he pressed his lips against hers and, when opened her mouth and accepted his tongue, his decision was made.

"Listen to me, love," he said as he broke the kiss and stared deep into her eyes. "Even if you don't agree with what I'm 'bout to say, which you probably won't, this is somethin' we will discuss only one time."

She quickly nodded. "Okay, baby."

"An' I need you to promise me that you won't repeat a word of this to anyone. Not even Tonya."

She kissed him softly on the lips. "Promise."

Knowing he was about to commit a major violation, JBo lowered his head and took a deep breath. "A'ight, look. When me and Juan-Juan was in the feds, he had this dre—"

"Death before dishonor, I put that on my momma. Shine in all my pictures, Rozay and nem swishers... "

"Don't answer it!" Olivia said as she latched on to his arm to prevent him from reaching for his phone.

"I got to. He already know I'm expectin' his call." Despite her disapproving glare, he answered. "What up, bra?"

"I'm here."

"A'ight, I'm on my way."

Olivia went ham when he hung up. "Are you fucking kidding me?"

"This business, love. I need you to understand that. When the time is right, I won't leave a stone unturned. Now, come here," he said as he tried to pull her into an embrace.

She swatted his hands away. "Don't touch me!"

"Livy—"

"No!" She took a step back as tears began to roll down her cheeks. "Please, just leave."

JBo paused at the front door and spoke without turning around. "Because there's so much you don't know about my past, you could never understand the position I'm in. But just know that I love you beyond words, and I need you in my life more than you can imagine."

Inside the Crown Vic, he fired up a Mild and just sat there for a minute, taking soothing pulls. When he finally brought the engine to life, his eyes were drawn to Olivia's bedroom window, where he found her staring out at him. As she silently pleaded for him not to leave, he felt like his heart was being slowly pulled from within his chest. Forcing himself to look away, he threw the car in drive and eased off; a single tear escaping from his eye as Wale and Usher's "The Matrimony" played through the speakers.

"If there's a question of my heart, you got it. It don't belong to anyone but you. If there's a question of my love, you got it. Baby, don't worry I got plans for you."

* * *

Juan-Juan was perched on the trunk of the Hyundai when JBo wheeled into his complex.

Emerging from the car, he smiled in an attempt to mask his inner distress. "What's good, my nigga?" He greeted as they slapped hands.

"Shit," Juan-Juan replied while eyeing him closely.

As they were walking toward his apartment, Juan-Juan suddenly froze in his tracks, causing JBo to stop and glance over his shoulder with a questioning look. "Wassup, bra?"

His expression serious as HIV, he asked, "Did you tell her?"

Shocked by the question, because he knew exactly what he was referring to, JBo shook his head. "Naw, my nigga, I ain't tell her."

Juan-Juan studied his eyes for a trace of dishonesty, then duly cautioned him, "Tighten up, fam."

Kweli

CHAPTER 13
Three Days Later

Juan-Juan was sprawled out on his bed, watching *Shottas* for the hundredth time when JBo blew off in his room. "Get up and get dressed, my nigga. You know what time it is."

Armed with $30,000 apiece, they jumped in JBo's Chevelle and flew to the mall. After dropping close to $6,000 up in Nordstrom on outfits and footwear, they went to cop chains from Mohammed— an Arab jeweler who played both sides.

It was love at first sight when JBo laid eyes on a thick-ass yellow-gold Cuban flooded with VVS's. Placing the weighty chain around his neck, he turned to Juan-Juan. "What you think, my nigga?"

He nodded in approval.

As they were waiting for Mohammed to finish counting the money, Juan-Juan noticed JBo's eyes kept darting toward a gold Presidential Rollie with a 30-pointer bezel. Reaching into his pockets, he pulled out every dollar he had and laid it on the counter.

JBo turned to face him with a slight frown. "That bitch twenty bucks, my nigga."

Juan-Juan nodded.

"But what about you? You ain't cop nothin' yet."

Pleased by his concern, Juan-Juan smirked. "Do you, fam."

* * *

"Dr. Patterson, please report to the nurse's station."

"Thank you." Olivia smiled at the nurse before going to take a seat in the waiting room.

As Dr. Patterson was approaching the nurse's station, his tired eyes instantly brightened at the sight of his beautiful daughter. *Our little girl's growing up, Vivian.* Because he knew her like the back of his hand, he could tell something was troubling her as soon as their eyes met. "Hey, baby girl, is everything okay?"

"I'm fine, daddy. But can we go somewhere and talk?"

As they sat across from each other in the hospital's cafeteria, Olivia began her spiel. "I want you to know that you could not have been a better father. Even when mom died, you still managed to give me enough comfort and support to help me get through it. And I know how deeply affected you were by it. For that, your strength is admirable. And because I love you and respect you as much as I do, I would never do anything to intentionally hurt or disappoint you." She reached across the table and grasped his hands. "As a favor to me, I'm asking you to give Javonte another chance."

He tensed up at the mention of his name.

She quickly continued, "He really wants to change his life, daddy. He got his GED and took some college courses while he was in prison. And now that he's out, he's going to enroll at Owens and start looking for a job." She soothingly rubbed the back of his hand with her thumb. "I would just like for there to be some type of communication between the two most important men in my life."

"Sweetheart, please listen to me." Knowing this was a touchy subject, he had to choose his words carefully. "For you to pursue a relationship with that young man is a risk not worth taking. Because in the end, it will only result in some type of heartache."

"But I love him, daddy. And I know he genuinely loves me, too. And with the right support, I know he can change his lifestyle. If you would just get to know him, then you'd see for yourself that he has a good heart."

"I'm not disputing that, Livy. But there are certain things you don't understand."

"Like what?" She questioned with a touch of sass.

"Like, how hard it'll be for him to totally disassociate himself from something he's been involved in all his life. Like how, if ever a choice had to be made, his allegiance to those streets would come before you. Like—"

"You talk as though he's incapable of changing."

"No, I'm not saying that. All I'm saying is that you can't possibly expect him to transform overnight."

"Why are you so hard on him? It's not like his life has been easy."

Dr. Patterson quickly shook his head. "I will not tolerate that as an excuse for a person's behavior. My upbringing was nowhere near Huxtable-like, but that did not prevent me making something of myself."

Raised by a single mother, Derrick Patterson had been raised on the crime infested and poverty-stricken west side of the city. Despite the unlawful actions of his surrounding peers, he had chosen a different route; refusing to become another statistic. Through perseverance and diligence, along with a vision, he graduated from high school with a full scholarship to the University of Toledo. Eight years later he was practicing medicine at St. Vincent's hospital as an ER physician.

Olivia released her father's hand and rose from the table. "I came here hoping you'd be more understanding and supportive. But it's clear I won't be receiving either. You have a good night, dad."

As he silently watched her leave, he was longing for the presence of his late wife. *Viv, you would've been so much better at this*. Although she had been gone nearly ten years from a painful bout with cancer, there was not a day that passed when he didn't think of her. Having been together since middle school, they could communicate without speaking, and would regularly finish each other's sentences. Her death was something from which there would never be a full recovery.

While Dr. Patterson rode the elevator back upstairs, he made a mental reminder to call his daughter when he got off work. *Don't worry, darling. I won't give up on our little girl.*

* * *

"Hello."

"It's JBo, Burg. I'm ready."

"Be at my office in an hour," he replied before disconnecting the call. For $4,000 and a vow to be responsible, he had agreed to let JBo borrow one his toys for the night.

"We 'bout to shit on niggas!" he excitedly told Juan-Juan as he hopped back on the E-way and made the Flowmaster scream.

Kweli

CHAPTER 14

Nearly every weekend, during and after club hours, people from all over the city would assemble at a plaza called Swaynefield. Whether you wanted to put a new whip on display, bag a bad bitch, or was a vulture on the prowl for an easy lick, then this was an event you were sure to attend. It was almost 2AM and, with nearly a hundred cars scattered throughout the parking lot, Swaynefield was jumping.

A large crowd was noisily standing around a high-stakes dice game when the unmistakable sound of gunfire rang out in the distance. As heads fearfully swiveled in different directions, a royal-blue Drophead Phantom came tearing down the street, dangerously weaving in and out of traffic. Being driven like a bucket, the car was approaching the intersection of Monroe and Detroit when the driver simultaneously slammed on the brakes and jerked the wheel to the left, causing the half-a-million dollar machine to drift into the turn.

Slowly, the 2014 Double-R crawled into the parking lot and came to a halt. With the crowd's undivided attention, the driver pressed a button inside the Drophead and the suede top began to retract. A Jeezy anthem was blaring from the 1000-watt Bang and Olufsen audio system.

"Got suede on ya' roof and ya' sittin' on leather... so many hunids in ya' pockets, them bitches startin' to stick together. Took them penitentiary chances and I rolled wit' that shit... knowin' damn well they find it, they gon' pose wit that shit."

In Louie Vuitton from head-to-toe, JBo pushed the door open and casually stepped out. His long-sleeve satin shirt was purposely left unbuttoned; the VVS's dancing in the Cuban as it laid against his muscular chest. His matching slacks— which hung a few inches below the band of his briefs, fell perfectly overall— and white loafers.

With a bottle of Louie in hand, and the Rollie commanding attention, JBo's hazel eyes arrogantly peered from behind white Carti's as he struck several poses for the cameras. He then trespassed into the personal space of a thick ass dime piece and handed her his bottle. While holding her stare, he removed a stack of blue faces from his pants pocket and carelessly flung it into the air. As both genders scrambled for the shower of loose bills, he snatched the bottle back and greedily chugged from it; allowing cognac to run freely down his chin.

As Juan-Juan stood in all-black Gucci and watched over him while he entertained the crowd, a light breeze parted the bottom of his linen shirt and exposed the pearl handle of a 1911, commonly known as The General. He wore a thin smirk, as it genuinely pleased him to see his mans enjoying himself.

Although Juan-Juan's alertness was turned up to the max as he stood guard, he failed to pick up on a pair of scheming eyes that were watching him and JBo from a distance.

In a freshly-stolen Chevy' Caprice, D-Wub swooped up in Swaynefield and parked at the far end of the plaza. Minutes later the female from the beauty salon hurriedly slid into the passenger seat and slouched down. As she took in his dark clothing and leather-gloved hands, there was no doubt as to what his intentions were.

D-Wub reached under the seat and grabbed a small brown paper bag. "I was startin' to think you ain't wont this lil' shit," he said as he tossed the 2-thousand in her lap.

* * *

Lightweight tipsy off the liquor, JBo was spitting flame at a female admirer when his phone began vibrating. Seeing Olivia's name on the screen, he excused himself before slurring into the phone, "What's up, love? Where you at?"

"Behind you," she answered sharply enough to let him know she had been posted up for a minute.

JBo spun around and saw her and Tonya standing next to the Hellcat. He smiled into the phone. "I'm glad you could make it."

"You sure about that? 'Cause it look like I might have been interrupting something."

Turned on by her jealousy, he gave her outfit a lustful once-over as he recited a line by the singer Drake. "Who told you to put them jeans on?"

Forcing herself not to smile, she looked away from him as he bopped toward her, rapping along the way.

When he got within arm's reach he hung up and pulled her into an embrace. Intoxicated by the fragrance of her Chanel Number 5 perfume, he buried his face into her neck and deeply inhaled. "Damn, girl, you smellin' gooder than a muthafucka."

"Whatever," she sassed, continuing to feign an attitude, although pleased by his compliments. "I saw you with that girl all up in your face."

"That was a harmless error, love," he said as he playfully put on a puppy-dog expression.

Unable to resist, she burst out laughing. "Boy, you so silly, you know that?"

Before some type of drama could unfold, which was usually how a night at Swaynefield ended, JBo suggested that they get in traffic. "Follow me," he told Olivia before turning to walk off.

Knowing he had been drinking, she quickly grabbed his arm. "Baby, I don't think you should be getting behind the wheel, so just let Tonya ride with Juan-Juan and you come with me." Before he could protest, she sucked his bottom lip into her mouth and boldly grabbed his dick; which instantly responded to her touch. "Do as I say, now," she whispered into his ear, "and I'll do as you say when we get home."

Without giving it a second thought, he tossed Juan-Juan the keys and went around to the passenger side of the Hellcat.

* * *

"Time for That" by Kevin Gates softly crooned the speakers as Juan-Juan navigated the spaceship out of the parking lot. Sunk into the ventilated seats with her feet planted on lamb's wool floor mats, Tonya took a minute to gaze up in amazement at the stars in the ceiling. She then turned in her seat and positioned herself to where she could focus squarely on Juan-Juan. "So, why haven't you been returning my calls?" When he offered no response, she smacked his arm. "Answer me!"

He snatched his eyes off the road and pinned her with a deadly stare.

"What?" Tonya challenged him. "I'm not scared of you. You might get that shit off with these niggas out here, but I know better."

"You don't know shit about me."

"I know yo' tough ass too scared to come from out of that emotional room you done barricaded yo' self in. And I also know that if you continue living like that, you gon' miss out on what we both know you in desperate need of... the love of a woman." Seeing by his facial expression that her words were having an effect, she continued, "I don't care about yo' past, or how ruined you think you are. I'm not going away, Juan-Juan. So, whether you like it or not, you just gon' have to deal wit' me."

When he glanced at her, she saw something in his eyes that warmed her heart. Vulnerability. As they came to a stop at a traffic light, she took advantage of the moment and leaned over and pressed her lips against his until he opened his mouth and accepted her tongue. And much to her surprise, he returned the kiss with equaled passion.

BOK! BOK! BOK! BOK! BOK! BOK! BOK! BOK!

Tonya released an agonizing cry into his mouth as hollow-points shattered the passenger side window and lodged themselves into her back.

The V-12 exhaled a monstrous roar as Juan-Juan smashed the gas. When he smacked the back of the car in front of him, D-Wub continued to squeeze as he maneuvered his way around to the driver's side of the Phantom.

BOK! BOK! BOK! BOK! BOK! BOK! BOK!

Moving with the quickness necessary for survival, Juan-Juan untangled himself from Tonya's lifeless body and scrambled out through the passenger's side. Lying on the ground, he extended his hand beneath the car and fired five shots in a sweeping motion.

BLOOM! BLOOM! BLOOM! BLOOM! BLOOM!

"Aaahhhh!" D-Wub hollered out as he almost buckled from a .45 slug that chewed into the lower part of his left leg. Forced to retreat, he angrily emptied his clip at the Phantom while hobbling off toward the Caprice.

As Juan-Juan helplessly watched the shooter skirt off in the burgundy-colored car, he could feel his life gradually slipping from within his grasp. He held only one regret as he began to lose consciousness. Not having the opportunity to stare his killer in the eyes.

CHAPTER 15

After fleeing the scene, D-Wub had hopped on the E-way and drove to a hospital on the outskirts of the city. Because the bullet went straight through, once a doctor stitched him up and lessened the pain with a Pere 10, he was able to limp out of the emergency room before the police could arrive with a million questions.

He was now seated in Kool-Aid's living room with his injured leg propped up on the coffee table.

"I can't believe this shit!" Kool-Aid vented in frustration as he stood across from him, smoking a cancer stick. "Not only can you tell me whether or not the nigga dead, but you done fuck around and let 'im shoot you in yo' got-damn leg!"

"I'm sayin', Gotti," D-Wub spoke through gritted teeth. "How the fuck I'm supposed to know he gon' be all hugged up wit' some bitch at the light?"

Kool-Aid shook his head stubbornly. "I ain't in the mood for no excuses, Wub. It's been damn near a month and you ain't bodied either one of these niggas." He eyed him with a distasteful expression and added, "Maybe they outta yo' league."

"Ain't no nigga on this earth outta my league!"

"I can't tell." Kool-Aid smirked as he looked down at D-Wub's injured leg. "'Cause you 'bout to have niggas out here lookin' at you like a straight clown."

D-Wub winced in pain as he rose up from the couch. "I'ma holla at you later on, Blood, 'cause I see you on some other shit right now."

As he was limping toward the front door, he withdrew a Glock-21 with blinding speed and shot Kool-Aid in the middle of his forehead.

BOK!

The 300-pounds of dead weight loudly collapsed to the floor in an awkward position.

"Nigga, who the fuck is you to question my murder-game?"

BOK!

"Like my shit ain't official!"

BOK!

"Like I ain't the only reason niggas ain't devoured yo' soft-ass!"

BOK!

After literally destroying Kool-Aid's face, he bent down and plucked the cigarette from between his fingers. "Now look at you," he said as he took a toke. "Up in this bitch smellin' like shit an' piss."

When D-Wub returned from the basement minutes later with a shopping bag containing a brick of Heroin and $36,000, he paused at the front door and gave the dead man a final glance. "You wasn't built to lead a wolf-pack no way."

* * *

When his eyes slowly blinked open, he looked around in confusion and slight panic until he saw JBo laying on a chair in the corner of the room. Realizing where he was, Juan-Juan tried to sit up and groaned loudly.

JBo instantly woke up and rushed to his bedside. "Hol' up, my nigga," he cautioned as he gently helped him lay back down. "You gon' have to chill for a minute."

He had been shot four times during the deadly encounter last night; the most fatal being one that nearly pierced his heart.

"How I get here?" he asked in a raspy voice. His last memory was of the shooter making a U-turn before driving off.

"They said you drove, then crashed into an ambulance outside in the parking lot."

While Juan-Juan had been stretched out on the pavement, leaking from his gunshot wounds, his mind warned him that if he allowed himself to pass out, his nap would be endless. So, through pure willpower and gritted teeth, he forced his body to get up off the ground and stagger toward the Phantom; which had coasted into the curb on the other side of the street.

A thick ass nurse entered the room as JBo was telling him that he had went back and found his gun. Her blue eyes widened in surprise when she looked up from her chart. She was not expecting to see a man who flat-lined twice last night suddenly up and talking. "I should go get the doctor," she said before turning to leave.

Knowing the police would also be notified, Juan-Juan advised JBo to get missing. "You know they 'bout to call them peoples, fam, so just gone and dip, and I'll see you in a few days."

As JBo was standing outside the hospital, waiting for Olivia to scoop him up, he got a call from Fat-Cat.

"Wassup, my nigga? You straight?"

"Yeah, I'm good."

"How the fam'?"

"He good."

"That's wassup," he said from the heart. "But check this out. Meet me up at the KFC on Bancroft real quick. I'm on my way there right now."

When Olivia pulled up minutes later, JBo could tell from her disheveled appearance and bloodshot eyes that she had not been to sleep. He pulled her into his arms and planted a kiss her forehead. "It's gon' be a'ight, love."

She gave a weak nod. "I just can't believe Tonya is actually dead." The harsh reality of how someone could be around one day, then suddenly gone the next, brought back painful memories of her mother.

As JBo went in her purse in search of a Black and Mild, he told her to shoot him over to the KFC. "Then, I'ma need you to stop by the mall so I can get Juan-Juan some new clothes. You know they had to cut all his shit off last night."

Fat-Cat was sitting behind the wheel of a Delta 88 when Olivia turned into the parking lot.

"I'll be right back," JBo said as he passed her the Mild. Ten minutes later he stumbled back to the car in a daze.

"What's wrong, baby?" Olivia inquired, noticing his troubled expression. Slowly shaking his head, he stared out the front windshield and mumbled, "Everything."

* * *

The detectives showed up while Juan-Juan was watching a Sanford and Son re-run. He smirked as he recognized them as being the same two that handled he and JBo's murder investigation.

"Well, well, well," Sterling chuckled as he closed the door and put his back against it. "Looks like someone was on the receiving end this time around."

Poker-faced, Juan-Juan continued to watch TV.

Spryzak stepped forward with a tape recorder. "How about giving us a detailed statement of what happened last night."

His version of events were simple— he couldn't recall anything beyond the point of leaving Swaynefield.

"You really think you're a tough motherfucker, don't you?" Sterling asked as he approached the bed in a threatening manner. "Well, let me tell you something, asshole. I'll kick your—"

Before he could boil over, Spryzak wedged himself between him and Juan-Juan. "Get a hold of yourself, Dan," he scolded the younger man. "We're in a fucking hospital for Christ sakes."

Too short to see over him, Sterling looked around him and pointed at Juan-Juan. "I'm gonna nail your black ass before I leave this earth, and that's a promise."

Showing no emotion, Juan-Juan's eyes never left the TV screen. He hated rats and was allergic to pork.

Kweli

CHAPTER 16

Olivia was standing over the stove, fixing dinner when JBo suddenly walked up and leaned against the kitchen's doorway. "I've been keepin' a lot of secrets from you, love."

Not knowing what to expect, since this was the first time he had spoken since they left KFC, she turned to face him with a nervous expression. "Like what, baby?"

He first admitted that the accusations she heard about him in the beginning were true. Yes, he and Juan-Juan did kill people, and had been doing so for quite a while. "But most times, money was the motive." Next, he told her about knocking Ciara down in exchange for the lick up in Detroit. "But that was strictly business and nothin' more." He then gave a full and unedited version of Juan-Juan's dream and what they intended to do. "It's gon' be murder... mayhem... and madness."

Olivia was speechless. While she found the violence disturbing, she was more unsettled by the fact that he had recently slept with another woman.

Before her lips could form a response, he was moved into her personal space. "Now that you know all my secrets," he calmly spoke into her ear, "tell me yours, 'cause we a team, remember?"

She shook her head while flashing an uneasy smile. "I don't have any secrets, baby. You know everything about me."

He looked away and smirked, as if that was the answer he was expecting. "Then who the fuck is D-Wub, bitch?" he screamed in pure rage.

Her facial expression was all the confirmation he needed.

When JBo had hopped inside the car with Fat-Cat, he listened to him explain how he was selling pills to a thot at Swaynefield last night when he saw Olivia duck off into a car with D-Wub. "You already know how the streets talk, my nigga," Fat-Cat said as he split a Swisher and emptied the guts into the ashtray. "So, everybody and they momma know Kool-Aid and 'nem want some get-back for that move at Glass City. So, when I heard about what happened to Juan-Juan and I thought about yo' girl creepin' behind enemy lines, I felt it was only right that I put a good man up on game."

Praying Fat-Cat gave the wrong answer, JBo asked him what color car it was.

"A burgundy Caprice."

Damn. The same color Juan-Juan said he saw the shooter skirt off in.

Feeling a mixture of anger and confusion, JBo grabbed Olivia by the neck and slammed her into the refrigerator. "Bitch, you tried to get me killed?"

She vigorously shook her head. "No, baby. It wasn't like that."

"Fuck you mean it wasn't like that? My nigga laid up in a hospital right now, and I coulda been in the car wit' 'im." He knew from Juan-Juan that Tonya was the only reason he was still alive.

"I would never have put your life in danger. Whether you had been drinking or not, I would have still convinced you to get in the car with me."

He frowned as he suddenly caught on to the underlying meaning of her statement. "So, what you sayin'? This was somethin' personal against Juan-Juan?"

"Do you know how much it hurts me to know that my love for you is not enough to compete with your loyalty to him? It spoils my appetite, and sometimes I can't even sleep at night. And not only that. It's like you actually have the potential to be something in life, but it's as if you're willing to follow him right into a graveyard instead. You were so focused on getting out and going to school and, regardless of what you say, I know he's the reason you put your plans on the backburner."

He eyed her in disbelief. "So, it gave you the right to try to get 'im killed?"

She lowered her head and mumbled, "No."

"An' how the fuck you meet this nigga D-Wub anyway?"

She told him about their encounter at the beauty salon. "I saw an opportunity and I went for it." She then looked up at him with genuine regret in her eyes. "But now that's it's all said and done, I realize that my rash decision was a terrible mistake." Although she had never imagined D-Wub would attempt the assassination at a traffic light, or in such a reckless manner, she knew she would forever shoulder the blame for Tonya's death.

"So, where the money at?"

"I didn't take it, 'cause it wasn't about that."

JBo looked away and slowly shook his head. He was unable to believe that she was capable of such a malicious and premeditated act.

"Baby," Olivia pleaded as she reached for his face.

He smacked her hand away. "Man, watch out."

"I'm sorry, Javonte, but I just couldn't stand by and continue to watch the man I love march down a self-destructive path. I know you and Juan-Juan have been through a lot together, but you've outgrown that part of your life. You are nothing like him. Your heart is not as cold. Why can't you see that?"

"Regardless of how you dress it up, that still don't give you the right to do what you did, Olivia."

"Do you know why it was so easy for me to stay loyal to you while you were locked up?"

Despite being heated, he couldn't help but glance at her in curiosity.

"Because I know with a certainty that you are the only man for me. You are irreplaceable, and not even my own father can stop me from being with you. Since losing my mother, you are the best thing that has happened to me, and I just can't imagine my life without you in it. I need you, Javonte." When she reached for him again and he didn't pull away, she went on to pour out her soul. "If you could see inside my heart, then you would know that I cherish you more than my next breath. When you told me about your childhood, I wanted nothing more than to protect you and love you with everything inside of me. My only fear was that I wouldn't be able to love you enough. But I vowed to myself that as long as I had oxygen in my body, I would never give up on you. I am a firm believer in what the Bible says: 'Love endures all, and it never fails.' Baby, I know I've made a terrible mistake, and you may never forgive me for it. But please understand that my only intention was to guard your well-being. And I speak directly from my heart when I say that all I want to do is give you the love, support and stability that you've never had."

Against his will, her spiel managed to bring tears to his eyes. *This shit unreal*, he thought as he clasped his hands on top of his head and stared at the ceiling.

Olivia wordlessly went to her knees and began to unfasten his pants. When she drew him into her hot mouth and tried to commit suicide by repeatedly stabbing her tonsils with the head of his dick, he silently cursed himself as he closed his eyes and surrendered to his lower-desires.

* * *

SMACK! SMACK! SMACK! SMACK! SMACK!

Olivia was screaming senselessly as JBo had her balled up in a pretzel like position and delivered a manhandling performance that was worthy of being on screen.

After spilling his seeds down her throat, he had drug her upstairs to her room and literally threw her on the bed. "Get naked!" he ordered while hastily removing his own clothes. Playing no games with the pussy, he came straight out the gate on some savage shit.

She clawed at his back and whatever else she could get her hands on, screamed for mercy until her voice went hoarse, and desperately tried to break loose. But he continued to punish her until the point of exhaustion.

As he began to slow down before eventually coming to a stop, her eyes opened and tears slowly trickled from their corners. She reached up and tenderly caressed his face, already forgiving him for the excessive force. "I'm sorry, Javonte," she sincerely apologized as she cradled his face in her hands. "And I love you so much, baby."

JBo just nodded as a tear fell from his eye and blended in with her own. Without a word, he then got out of bed, grabbed a Mild off the nightstand and left the room.

Olivia was sound asleep when he returned thirty-minutes later. He quietly got dressed, allowing his tears to flow as he watched the steady rise and fall of her chest and listened to the light snore he had grown to love.

Leaning down, he gently kissed her forehead and whispered, "I love you, too."

BOC!

The gunshot was immediately followed by an agonizing cry as the gun fell from JBo's hand and he slowly collapsed to his knees. Squeezing the sheets inside his fists, he buried his face into the bed and cried like a baby. He had just killed the only woman he would ever love.

CHAPTER 17

Juan-Juan was coming out of the bathroom when Amber, the blue-eyed nurse, softly knocked before entering his room. She shot him a questioning look, to which he shook his head. He was being released in a few hours and still had not heard anything from JBo.

Aside from the healing process, the past two weeks had been torturous, because not only was JBo MIA, but he and Olivia's phones were going straight to voicemail. He knew something was wrong, and the endless possibilities drove him crazy.

"So, what are you gonna do?" Amber inquired, secretly wishing he would turn to her for assistance. Having grown fond of him during his two-week stay, the young white girl couldn't resist her attraction to his masculine and mysterious nature.

"Just get my shit ready and call a cab."

Stung by his sharp reply, she lowered her head and quickly left the room.

Juan-Juan went over to his window and stared out at the city with a worried expression. *Where you at, my nigga?*

* * *

After walking down a nickel in the feds, T-Woods was finally back on Cleveland soil. He stepped off the Greyhound and flashed a broad smile when he saw Ham leaning against his car, smoking a cancer-stick. "Boy, if you don't get yo' lil' Kevin Hart looking ass up outta here!"

129

Ham came off the car and fired right back. "If you don't get yo' Caesar off the Planet of Apes looking ass up outta here!"

Both men joined in laughter as they slapped hands and embraced.

"What's good, lil' nigga?" T-Woods asked.

"I'm coolin'."

"So, wassup? You heard from that nigga Juan-Juan yet?"

Ham shook his head. "That nigga either back locked up or somewhere takin' a dirt nap."

Visibly disappointed, T-Woods looked away and cursed under his breath. With only a few crumbs on his debit card, and not nearly enough job experience to secure anything over minimum wage, he had needed this lick more than a person on dialysis needed a kidney transplant.

When they got inside the car, a 2000 beige Lincoln, Ham told T-Woods not to panic as he brought the engine to life. "I got a lil' move we can put down on the west side. Some square-ass nigga name Rico be trappin' out a spot 'cross the street from my baby momma. And from what she say, the nigga soft as cotton. So, this should be a walk in the park."

Since his release nearly two weeks ago, Ham had already pulled off a few minor stick-ups, while doing surveillance on Rico that would have impressed an FBI agent.

"So, when you tryna do it?" T-Woods anxiously inquired. It might not have been the lick he was looking forward to, but it would be something to at least keep his knuckles from dragging the ground.

"Shid, tonight. We gone wait till like one in the mornin', then run up in that bitch like Zeke-the-Freak, you feel me?"

T-Woods eyed him with a predatory look as they clapped up. "Let's eat!"

Ham threw the car in drive and was about to pull off until he noticed a navy-blue Yukon creeping through the parking lot. His heart instantly started knocking when it stopped directly in front of them.

T-Woods cut his eyes at him and hissed, "Fuck you done did, nigga?" Although there were no strobe-lights on the roof, he already knew who it was by the heavy tint and factory wheels.

Too nervous to respond, Ham could only think about the strap under his seat. *I ain't even been out a month*, he thought dreadfully to himself as his palms began to sweat. *Ain't no way I'm goin' back already*, he concluded as he slowly began reaching down.

T-Woods peeped his movements and started to reach for the door handle. *This nigga foolin'*.

When the driver's side window of the SUV lowered, both men exhaled in relief as they saw who was behind the wheel.

Ham hopped out the car. "Nigga, we thought—"

"Ain't no time for rappin' right now," JBo cut him off. "We gotta get on the road."

After Ham dropped the Lincoln off at his baby momma's, they took T-Woods to see his PO, then jumped on the E-Way, en route to Toledo.

* * *

"So, I guess this is it," Amber said to Juan-Juan as he opened the cab's back door. She had accompanied him outside in hopes that he would have a last-minute change of heart. She rose up on her tiptoes and kissed his cheek. "Take care of yourself."

"Likewise," Juan-Juan replied before he slid down into the cab and closed the door. He gave the driver the address to his apartment; not once looking back as they eased out of the parking lot.

As the cab was coming to a pause at a stop sign, the Yukon suddenly sped up next to it and the backdoor was pushed open. Juan-Juan smirked before handing the cab-driver a twenty. "I'ma get out right here."

"Wassup, my nigga?" JBo said as they locked eyes in the rear-view. "You ready?"

"Ain't no mystery."

He cut the music back up and sped off toward the airport where he had already copped four tickets in first-class.

"Ain't nothin' in life guaranteed," JBo had told T-Woods and Ham while on the way to pick up Juan-Juan. "So, you already know it's a chance shit can go sour, whether it be a coffin or a cage. So, before we make this move, we gon' go outta town and do it like bosses for a night."

While waiting for their flight, JBo leaned close to Juan-Juan and spoke in a hushed tone. "I can only imagine what the past two weeks done been like. But just know, it's been rough for me, too." The bags beneath his eyes and uncut hair were clear indications he was spilling facts. "But I'm sayin', let's just go down here and try to enjoy ourselves, then on the way back, I won't leave a stone unturned."

As the Boeing was ascending into the clouds, JBo recalled a promise they had made to themselves when they were being flown to Oklahoma on a federal plane. Wearing a thin smile, he nudged Juan-Juan with his elbow. "'Member we said we would fly in first-class one day?"

Kweli

CHAPTER 18

Courtesy of Wittenburg, they had the luxury of stepping off the plane at Atlanta International and hopping straight into a '14 G-Wagon. Diamond black with a panorama view, JBo slid behind the wheel and punched it to Western Union where he had had the lawyer wire $20,000.

Wittenburg had almost blew a gasket when he first learned about the damage done to his Phantom. But as he listened to the news of Tonya's death and Juan-Juan's critical condition, his temperature had gradually cooled. "Don't worry 'bout it, kid," he'd told JBo over the phone. "It's just a car. And with it being insured, I'll have new one in no time."

When JBo had showed at his office yesterday morning with a bag of money and several requests, Wittenburg— a true businessman— did not hesitate to make the necessary arrangements.

"GPS that Underground spot," Juan-Juan spoke up from the backseat as they were leaving Western Union.

The Underground was a local mall they heard about through a notorious car-thief at Manchester. "If y'all niggas ever come down my way, make sho' you find the Underground," Car-Jack had told them as they were standing in commissary one day. "An' holla at my lil' potnas that be sellin' CD's and shit. No exaggeration, they got access to whatever you need, shawty."

Juan-Juan went in alone and came back out minutes later with a young light-skinned nigga name Reese, who had a bad habit of constantly looking over his shoulders out of paranoia. He grabbed a bag from the trunk of a white bucket before they got inside a different car and made a quick exchange.

As Juan-Juan jumped back in the Benz, JBo wordlessly pulled off. What was understood didn't need to be explained.

They ate at Gladys Knight's— a chicken and waffle spot owned by the legendary singer— then went to Lennox mall to get fitted. Before going inside, JBo peeled Ham and T-Woods off $3,000 apiece. "Spend it all," he said as they counted the bills in disbelief.

Carrying bags full of designer clothes, they were leaving the mall when JBo stopped in front of a jewelry store and asked Ham and T-Woods if they wanted a chain.

"Hell yeah!" T-Woods answered without hesitation.

For $12,000, they both got a platinum chain and a decent-size cross with a few stones in it.

After getting crispy at a barber shop in Zone-6, they went to take showers and get dressed at the Marriott Marquee where a suite for each man had already been reserved. Two hours later, they were standing in the lobby, exchanging nods of approval toward each other's choice of attire.

JBo was in square-toe Mauri gators, linen slacks and a gold and black Versace shirt with a fedora cocked ace-deuce over his brush-waves. Ham came D-Boy in a Cleveland Cavs snapback, a fitted Givenchy v-neck, Balmain jeans encircled by a medusa-head Versace belt, and spiked hi-top Christian Louboutin's. T-Woods did it casual in a

Ferragamo button-up, Tom Ford jeans and Louis Leeman Italian leather dress shoes. Juan-Juan kept it simple but tasteful in a pair of navy-blue Foams, True Religion jeans and a $700 Balenciaga hoodie.

As they were marching across the parking lot toward the Wagon, Juan-Juan called Reese and told him he needed some pills. He gave him the name of a liquor store near the Underground and said to meet him there in thirty-minutes.

When they drove up to the store, instead of turning into the semi-crowded lot, JBo pulled around the corner and parked. "Like a robbery, my nigga," he told Juan-Juan as they locked eyes in the rear-view. "In and out."

"What he on?" Ham nosily questioned as he looked in his side mirror and watched Juan-Juan disappear around the corner.

Even T-Woods' ears perked up in curiosity as he waited for JBo's response. Before he could answer, three rapid gunshots rang out; causing both men to jerk their heads in the store's direction. They quickly turned back around and looked straight ahead as Juan-Juan came jogging back to the truck.

Pulling his hood off as he climbed in, he tossed a bag of pills and some Loud up front. "Had to make sho' it worked." He shrugged nonchalantly, speaking in reference to the gun he had bought earlier from the now deceased Reese.

As JBo calmly pulled away from the curb and cut the music back up, T-Woods stole a glance at him and Juan-Juan; suddenly realizing that he was in the presence of the devil's offspring. *These niggas vicious.*

* * *

By the time they arrived at the club, the Molly's had their eyes as bright as the yellow and purple Onyx sign. JBo recklessly sped into the parking lot and skidded to a stop; attracting the attention of everyone standing in line.

"Cut It" by O.T. Genesis blared from the Wagon's surround sound system as Ham hopped out and left the passenger door open. In a zone, he threw a Molly in the air, caught it in his opened mouth, then started dancing. His Chris Brown-like moves had the women feeling him, as they bobbed their heads and recited the lyrics to the song.

JBo paid a buck to leave the truck where it was, $400 to skip the long line, and another $400 to get in. As he was being wanded down, he discreetly slid a stack into the bouncer's hand and nudged his head at Juan-Juan. "He won't go nowhere without it."

When Juan-Juan stepped up, the big man avoided eye contact as he waved the deactivated wand up and down his body.

It was a mesmerizing sight when they set foot inside the spacious building. "Black Beatles" by Rae Sremmurd and Gucci Mane was booming through the speakers as multitudes of half-naked women strutted around the club.

T-Woods excitedly hit Ham on the arm and yelled over the music, "Nigga, you see this shit?" They had been to a few strip clubs in the past, but nothing of this caliber. So, to be standing in one known world-wide while rocking designer clothes and platinum chains was an experience they would never forget.

Once they were seated at a booth in VIP, a bow-legged waitress in spandex shorts approached their table and settled into a mean stance. "What y'all drankin' on?" she sang in a-southern accent.

T-Woods bit his bottom lip as he lustfully studied her thickness. The ass was so fat that he couldn't resist from grabbing it. "Damn!" He cried out as his fingers sank into its softness. He glanced up at her with a serious expression. "I'm tryna drank yo' bath water."

She cracked a slight grin as she removed his hand. "Boy, you somethin' else."

They went overboard, ordering bottles of Patron, 1738, Rose Moet, and different flavors of Ciroc which were strictly for the strippers.

"Turn this into singles for us, sweetheart," JBo said as he gave her a rubber-banded roll of blue faces.

Suddenly seeing dollar signs, she shot T-Woods a sensual look before walking off. Knowing she had his undivided attention, she nastily stomped toward the bar; making her loose cheeks jiggle every step of the way.

Their booth was swarmed by five strippers as bottles and stacks of singles were being delivered to their table.

When one of them stood in front of Ham and started twerking, he reached out and shoved her. "Bitch, get yo' plastic booty ass outta here! Fuck I look like spendin' real money on some fake shit?"

As one of the bouncers began to make his way over, he was intercepted by the bowlegged waitress who was now in stilettos and a purple thong. She whispered something in his ear, to which he nodded and returned to his post. Accompanied by three other stallions, she walked up to T-Woods and boldly crawled on his lap. Placing his hands on her ass cheeks, she started grinding to the music, causing him to instantly brick-up. Sour-faced, the other strippers stormed off with their middle fingers held high.

The waitress—who was also a part-time stripper—introduced herself and her three friends. "I'm Candy, and these my girls Mee-Mee, Kitty and Redd."

Ham was flashing all thirty-two as he came face-to-face with Mee-Mee's authentic measurements. He smacked her on her fat ass, then pointed at it while looking around. "Now this what the fuck I'm talkin' 'bout!"

As Kitty paired up with JBo, Redd went and stood between Juan-Juan's legs. They stared each other down for a minute before she slowly straddled his lap. "I know yo' kind," she said as they continued to maintain eye contact.

He quickly grabbed her wrist as she reached toward the small of his back.

Guiding his hand inside her red thong, she brushed his knuckles across the fat lips of her gushy pussy and purred into his ear, "Young nigga, I love that gangsta shit."

The club turned up when the DJ played Rihanna's stripper's anthem, "Pour it Up". Money rained like confetti as the dancers went berserk;

trying to outdo each other with different ass-clapping and flexibility techniques.

While chugging Patron straight out the bottle, Ham used his phone to record T-Woods and JBo as they stood over the strippers and awarded them for their creative performances. By the end of the song, the four women were standing ankle-deep in loose bills. Ham jumped up on the table and shouted, "Somebody get a rake up in this bitch!"

In less than five minutes, they had carelessly blown $10,000.

When JBo slid off to holler at the DJ, Ham and T-Woods went and took pictures for their comrades still behind the fence. As they struck a number of poses with various strippers, they made sure their chains were visible in every picture.

On his way back to the booth, JBo bumped into Candy and draped his arm around her neck. "Listen, Ma. I already know a woman like you tryna level up. So, I'm sayin', what's ticket gon' be for us foreigners to receive a lil' southern hospitality for the night?"

She thought over the proposition for a minute before asking, "Just me, or all of us?"

JBo chuckled. "Come on, sweetheart, I'ma grown ass man."

"Five thousan'. I'll split it four ways."

He kissed her cheek. "Say no more."

As they were leaving the building with four of the club's baddest strippers, the DJ stopped the music and illuminated them with a spotlight. "We got some Midwest playas in here, reppin' the state of Ohio. Y'all give it up for Juan-Juan, JBo, T-Woods, and Ham."

JBo raised his bottle as the crowd saluted, while Ham yelled out, "Cleveland or nothin'!"

"Get It in Ohio" by Cam'ron was blaring through the club as they made their exit.

"Nigga, I'm finna punish this hoe!" T-Woods boasted as they drove out the parking lot. He hit the weed and held it. "She'on know a nigga been gone for a nickel, and ain't jacked off in like a year." He exhaled a Kush cloud toward the ceiling. "Shid, nigga, I'm 'bout to go harder than Brian Pumper up in this mu'fucka."

Laughter erupted inside the truck as they swerved through traffic with the women trailing behind them in Candy's Buick Lacrosse.

***

When getting back to the Marriott, they clapped-up before leading the women off to their individual suites.

Ham skipped the foreplay and jumped straight to the main event. With his hat turned backwards and shoes laced up as tight as boxing gloves, he had Mee-Mee in front of a large mirror. For an extra $500, he had convinced her to let him go bare-face. Making her bend over and grab her ankles, he spat on the head of his dick, then viciously plunged into her.

"Aaaahhhh!" She screamed at the top of her lungs as her head slammed into the mirror.

"Yeah, you thought shit was sweet, huh? Thought 'cause a nigga was small he couldn't get up in these guts, huh?" He sucked his thumb, then stuck it in her ass. "I'ma show you how a Cleveland nigga get down tonight, bitch!"

142

* * *

Kitty was kneeling between JBo's legs, bobbing her head while he sat on the bed staring off into space. His mind was being held hostage by memories of Olivia. The flashbacks were triggered when Kitty cut on the radio and one of her favorite songs by Beyoncè came on.

After nearly fifteen minutes of slurping, slobbering and spitting on JBo's limp dick, Kitty angrily rose to her feet and started picking up her clothes. "Since you obviously can't rise to the occasion, I'ma go see if I can join one of my girls."

Her words struck a nerve, causing JBo to jump up and grab her arm. Although he would never see her again, he refused to let her belittle his manhood. Forcing Olivia to the back of his mind, he led Kitty back over to the bed and pushed her down.

She hungrily eyed his dick as he stroked it into an erection before placing an Ultra-Thin condom over it. "What you thank you 'bout to do wit' that?"

He grabbed his bat and stepped up to the plate. "I'm 'bout to teach yo' disrespectful ass some manners."

* * *

Redd had Juan-Juan hemmed up against the wall as she massaged his dick through his jeans and teasingly licked his lips. "You can pretend I'm her if you want to."

He shot her look, knowing she couldn't possibly mean what he thought she did.

She nodded. "Yeah, I see the way you been lookin' at me all night, like I remind you of somebody from yo' past."

In that moment, he came to regard Redd with a certain level of respect, because it was true. He did notice a strong resemblance between her and Tonya. Even their frames were alike.

When Redd squatted and began to unfasten his pants, Juan-Juan reached behind his back to remove the pistol. As he went to lay it on the counter, she grabbed his arm. While gazing up at him with a look of genuine desire, she circled her tongue around the head of his dick, then brought the .380 toward her mouth and licked its barrel. "Didn't I tell yo' young ass I love that gangsta shit?"

* * *

"Say I'm a beast!" T-Woods demanded as he manhandled Candy from the back with long and powerful strokes. He had been making her glorify his dick game every step of the way.

"You a beast!" she obediently cried out as her eyes rolled up into her head.

With thick, creamy juices trickling down the back of her thighs, she had lost count of the orgasms.

KNOCK! KNOCK! KNOCK! KNOCK! KNOCK!

T-Woods instantly froze in mid-stroke and nervously glanced over his shoulder. Those were not regular knocks.

KNOCK! KNOCK! KNOCK! KNOCK! KNOCK!

He signaled for Candy to be quiet, then crept to the door and looked through the peephole. Sighing in relief, he cracked the door open just enough to poke his head out. "Nigga, you—"

"Hurry up and get dressed. We gotta go," Ham whispered in an urgent tone while nervously looking up and down the hallway.

T-Woods frowned. "Fa what?"

"The bitch shitted on me, bra, and I freaked out."

As soon as Ham had replaced his thumb with his dick and started going crazy, Mee-Mee had tried to stop him. But, ignoring her warnings, he mashed her face into the pillow and continued to anally crush her. When he got ready to switch positions, he pulled out and doo-doo sprayed everywhere.

T-Woods eyed him in disbelief. "Is you serious?"

"As colon cancer."

"Where she at now?"

"Shid, in the room on some unconscious type shit. Hoe made it worse by tryna fight back."

T-Woods shook his head in disgust. If he had a strap right then, he might've fired Ham up right there in the hallway. "Hol' up, bra," he grumbled before closing the door.

As he hurriedly got dressed, he told Candy he would be right back. "This dumb ass nigga done lost his phone and I'ma help 'im look for it real quick."

After rounding up Juan-Juan and JBo, they piled inside the Benz and fled to the airport, where they were able to board an early flight back to Ohio.

Kweli

CHAPTER 19

"Olivia gone, fam," JBo quietly announced while looking down at the earth.

Juan-Juan frowned in confusion. "She gone?"

He slowly nodded. "I had to put her down."

Juan-Juan's eyebrows instantly rose. While he wasn't surprised by much, him taking her life was unimaginable.

JBo turned from the window and surprised him for a second time. "She was the reason you got shot."

While giving him a full rundown, his eyes got watery when he got to the part where he put one in her head, then later drove the body to a secluded area and buried it. "I ain't even gon' lie to you, my nigga. I really didn't even wonna do it. But on the strength of what our friendship represents, I knew I ain't have no choice."

JBo was the perfect example of someone who understood that when it comes to being real, there is no gray area. It's either you *is*, or you *ain't*. It's the decisions we make when confronted with tough choices that will determine who we truly are.

Guilt was eating away at Juan-Juan's insides as he thought about the secret he was keeping from a man whose loyalty had no boundaries.

JBo noticed his troubled expression. "Don't worry 'bout it, my nigga, 'cause I didn't do nothin' you wouldn't have done for me." His statement was referring to a situation back in '07, when they had been separated for nearly a year.

* * *

A few months after Ms. Teresa orchestrated their separation and had JBo moved to a different orphanage, he got adopted by Henry and Annette Carter— a married couple who had been together twenty-years.

Both in their late 40's, they had lost their own son, Henry Jr., to a hit-and-run when he rode his bicycle into the street. Because it happened under Annette's watch, Henry blamed her for the death of their only child. As time progressed, he evolved into a bitter and sometimes abusive alcoholic. To salvage her crumbling marriage, Annette came up with the idea of adoption. Despite Henry's protests, she badgered him into consent.

Needless to say, it didn't take JBo long to pick up on the strong dislike from his foster dad. Annette had tried to convince him that Henry's behavior was not personal, but rather, the result of how deeply affected he was by their son's death. "Just give him time, Javonte. He'll eventually come around."

Desperately wanting to be part of a family, JBo did everything he could to gain Henry's approval. But one evening he made it perfectly clear that he should never expect to be embraced as his biological son.

JBo had been playing Grand Theft Auto when Henry suddenly barged into his room. "You took the trash out yet?" he growled, smelling as if he had bathed in a tub full of liquor.

"Naw, not yet," he answered without taking his eyes off the screen.

"Well, you need to cut this damn game off and get it done. It's gettin' late."

"A'ight." He nodded as his thumbs continued to dance over the controller. "Just let me finish this part right here real quick."

Henry snatched the controller out of his hand and flung it. "I said do it now, got-dammit!"

Without thinking, JBo popped straight up off the bed. "Man, what the—"

Before he could finish the sentence, Henry clamped a monkey paw around his neck and slammed him into the wall. "Nigga, don't you ever disrespect me up in my muthafuckin' house! You understand me?" As JBo clawed at his fingers and struggled to breathe, Henry hurled him into the dresser. "Now go take out that muthafuckin' trash like I told you to."

With tears of anger and hurt threatening to spill from his eyes, JBo lunged forward and threw a wild punch. Having grown up in an era where learning how to fight came before learning to ride a bike, Henry easily slipped it and went down low with a vicious gut-shot. JBo cried out as he doubled over in pain. Showing no mercy, Henry buckled him with a hook to the kidney's that made his bladder release.

"Henry!"

Eyes wild with rage, he spun around to face his wife, who stood in the doorway with her hand covering her mouth in shock. She was staring at JBo as he lay curled up on the floor in a fetal position.

"Get yo' ass back downstairs, Annette!" Henry pointed with his index finger. "This here is man business!"

Trembling with fear, she cowardly obeyed.

After locking the door, Henry began taking off his leather belt. "So, you wanna put yo' hands on grown folks, huh?" It wasn't until he got exhausted did he stop striking JBo all over his body. With the X-Box tucked under his arm, Henry paused in the doorway and looked back without a trace of sympathy. "An' get yo' pissy ass in the shower after you take that trash out, too."

* * *

Four Months Later

Lil' Boosie was banging inside the stolen El-Camino as Juan-Juan drove to the mall to cop the new Jordan Retros. Expressionless, he steered with his left while the right rested in his lap, clutching the Trey-Five-Seven. Since they met, the two had stuck together like Siamese twins.

Juan-Juan had come a long way since the night he ended the dopefiend's career. No longer breaking in cars, he was now burglarizing houses on all four corners of the city; taking big-screens and whatever else of value he stumbled across. With the Arab store owner readily cashing him out, he was seeing close to $500 a week easily.

On one of the rare occasions she was home, his foster mother had caught him leaving the house one day and pulled him up. "Boy, where you get them expensive looking ass clothes from? 'Cause I know damn well I ain't bought none of that shit." When he didn't respond, she pointed her finger and threatened, "Don't forget I can send yo' lil' manish ass back to that place."

Knowing she was driven by greed, Juan-Juan calmly laid a big face on the table along with a compromise. "There's more where that came from if you stay the fuck outta my way."

Juan-Juan was high-stepping through the mall when he instinctively glanced over to the food court section. Pumping his brakes, he thought his eyes were deceiving him at first. But as he edged closer and got a better look, he felt a mixture of concern and excitement.

Seated at one of the tables was a woman with her head down and hands folded in her lap. Next to her sat a man whose eyebrows were furrowed into a tight frown as he stabbed at his salad. And across from them was JBo who wore a sad expression while picking over his food.

Feeling the intensity of someone's stare, JBo looked up. His eyes widened as he found himself staring at the friend he thought of on a daily basis. When Juan-Juan threw his hands up, he thought for a split-second, then politely excused himself from the table, saying he had to use the bathroom. Juan-Juan waited a minute before following behind him.

Inside the restroom, the two friends slapped hands and bear-hugged before a word was spoken.

Juan-Juan nudged his head at the door as they broke apart. "Wassup wit' that situation out there?"

Unable to maintain eye contact, JBo put his head down in shame.

Juan-Juan bent down. "Man, wassup?"

A tear fell as he mumbled, "My foster dad."

After the first beating, the others became frequent. Careful not to target anything above the neck, Henry would tear off into him for the slightest reason. "You'll never replace my son!" he would announce on a regular basis.

Annette, too afraid to intervene, convinced JBo to keep the abuse a secret. "I know it's tough, Javonte, but you'll be grown in a few years. So, unless you wanna go back to an orphanage, I suggest you tell them everything is fine when you have your review."

Without needing to hear anymore, Juan-Juan already knew what he was going through. He had experienced it himself. "Where you live at?" he asked JBo through gritted teeth.

As he was giving him the address, Henry stormed into the bathroom. "What's taking you so damn long up in here?"

"This my friend from school. I was just—"

"Well talk to him at school then, 'cause right now you need to get yo' stupid ass out here so we can go."

As they were walking out, Juan-Juan yelled, "Till I'm traced in chalk!"

Henry glanced back with a scowl, while JBo did something he had rarely been doing— smiled.

* * *

Juan-Juan pulled up to the yellow house at eleven that night and tapped the horn. A downstairs curtain moved, then seconds later JBo crept out the front door with a backpack slung over his shoulder and one in his hand.

Juan-Juan slid to the passenger's side and hopped out. He took the bags from JBo and tossed them in the car. "Where that nigga at?" he asked as he quietly closed the door.

"Let's just dip, my nigga."

He shook his head stubbornly. "You the only friend I ever had."

Not knowing Juan-Juan already had one under his belt, JBo led him into the house. His eyes got big when Juan-Juan removed the chrome revolver from behind his back.

"Stay right here," he whispered before he slowly turned the doorknob and slipped inside the room. He briefly watched as they peacefully slept beneath the covers, then flicked the light.

Annette woke up first. She shrieked in terror at the sight of the hooded figure standing in their room with a large pistol.

Henry tried to play tough as he protectively held on to his wife. "What the hell you want?"

To awaken his memory, Juan-Juan jumped up on the foot of their bed and pulled off his hood.

"You that lil' mean-eyed bastard from the mall earlier. Did Javonte put you up to this?" Feeling a surge of bravery, he threw the covers back and went to get up. "Where that lil' son-of-a—"

Juan-Juan lifted the cannon and froze his movements. "Lay yo' bitch-ass back down."

Seeing the devil in his eyes, Henry reluctantly obeyed. "If he told you we got money, he lied. I gotta few hundred in my wallet and that's it. So just take it and get the fuck outta here."

Juan-Juan smirked. "I ain't here for no money, old-head."

Henry frowned. "Then what the hell you want?"

In reply, he yelled out, "Aye, JBo!" When he hesitantly entered the room, Juan-Juan motioned for him to come closer. "Come face this coward, my nigga."

Henry blazed with anger as he and JBo locked eyes. "You better be glad he got that gun."

JBo spat in his face.

Before Henry could react, Juan-Juan gripped the Python in both hands and dogged him.

BOOM! BOOM!

Annette screamed as she was splattered with bloody fragments of her husband's skull.

"You shoulda stopped it," Juan-Juan condemned her, right before squeezing two in her face.

BOOM! BOOM!

JBo reached for the murder weapon as he jumped down from the bed.

Juan-Juan beamed in admiration when JBo turned and fired the last two shots; one in each body.

Hurriedly fleeing the scene, they got to the front door when JBo suddenly froze in his tracks. "I can't leave."

Not yet understanding, Juan-Juan looked at him crazy. "You can't leave?"

He quickly shook his head. "You know somebody done pro'ly called the police after all them loud ass shots. When they get here and I'm gone, I'ma be they first suspect." He put a hand on Juan-Juan's shoulder. "You gon' have to tie me up and hit me, then tear this bitch up and make it look like a burglary gone bad."

After he tied him up, gagged him, then hit him hard enough to make him bleed, Juan-Juan ransacked the house. Before leaving, he paused at the bottom of the stairs and looked back up at JBo's room. He understood his logic, but still hated to leave him behind.

Going out through the backdoor, he ran to the car and grabbed a crowbar, then went back and pried the door open. *See you in a minute, my nigga*, he said to himself as he ran back to the car and pealed out.

* * *

Sloppy drunk and alone, Michelle staggered into the house at 3AM. She gasped in surprise when she hit the light and saw Juan-Juan seated on the couch.

"Boy, you almost—" Her words got caught in her throat as she noticed the gun in his hand. *Her* gun.

Rising from the couch, he walked down on her until they were inches apart. "Tomorrow, you gon' call around and find out what orphanage Javonte Bowden in. Then, I want you to go adopt him. If you do it, you can have both checks for yo' self. But if you don't..." He pressed the barrel against her forehead. "I'ma blow this muthafucka off."

Instantly sober, Michelle's head quickly nodded in understanding. "I'll make it happen."

As she fearfully laid in bed that night with her eyes glued to her door, Michelle realized that this was not the same boy she had brought into her home eleven months ago. *Lord Jesus, I have a monster in my home.*

* * *

The 787 was landing back in Ohio when JBo asked Juan-Juan how he wanted to handle the D-Wub situation. "'Cause if you want to, my nigga, we can slide through the city real quick."

He shook his head. "Nah, let's just stay on track."

From the airport, where JBo had paid to leave the Yukon, they hopped on I-75. Headed to the state's capital, they were on their way to either becoming millionaires, co-defendant's, or tenants at the local cemetery.

CHAPTER 20

Chinx was playing low inside the silver 'Vette as it turned onto a dead-end street and glided down the block. Parking in front of a white house, the driver scanned the area before grabbing a bag off the passenger seat and hopping out; a 30-round Glock attached to his right hand.

With a noticeable limp and watchful eyes, D-Wub went around to the back of the house and knocked twice with the butt of his pistol. The door was opened seconds later and he disappeared inside.

Greeted by one of his flamed-up hooligans, Boob-Mac, he was led into a small kitchen where another man was seated at the table, chiefing on a stick of Strong.

"What's brackin', Wub?" Suge acknowledged with a head nod. "Big B's, Gotti."

"I know this better be 'bout some bread," Boob-Mac jokingly said to D-Wub as he took the blunt from Suge. "'Cause, nigga, I was in the middle of cradlin' this bad white bitch out in Maumee. On my momma, this hoe look like Demi Lovato."

D-Wub smirked as he sat the bag on the table along with his strap, then started getting undressed.

"Damn, Wub, wassup?" Boob-Mac questioned as he and Suge leaned back with their faces scrunched up.

He wordlessly continued removing his clothes.

They quickly turned their heads when he began taking off his briefs. "Come on, fam," Boob-Mac whined as he stared toward the front room.

Standing before them in his birthday suit, he finally spoke. "Get naked."

When they started mumbling in defiance, he snatched the strap up off the table. "Strip!" After making them slowly turn in a circle with their arms up, he unzipped the duffel bag and tossed two sweatsuits on the table. "Put them on." Stuffing their other clothes inside a trash bag, he had Suge throw it outside on the back porch.

"What was all that fo', Wub?" Boob-Mac inquired as they settled themselves around the kitchen table.

"Paranoia is sometimes priceless," he answered right before firing up a Newport King and bathing his lungs in the cancerous fumes. Exhaling a stream of smoke from his nostrils, he eyed both men with an intense stare and forewarned, "Y'all my two closest men, but if you repeat a word of what I'm 'bout to speak on, I'll treat you niggas like enemies."

Recalling a recent incident where they had personally witnessed the degree of his savagery, they quickly nodded in understanding.

* * *

Right after sending Kool-Aid off to the other side, D-Wub assembled the troops in the basement of a duck-off and announced that he was now acting as Commander-in-Chief. As he watched their various reactions, he added, "If anyone feels my decision is not what's best for the team, then now is the time to speak up."

Gator—a young boss who also had his eye on the throne— stepped forward and voiced his disapproval. "I'm sayin', Wub. No offense, but you a shooter, my nigga. Ride shotgun and let somebody else take the wheel."

D-Wub nodded as if he could understand his point-of-view. Then, while maintaining a mellow expression, he gracefully withdrew a .40 from beneath his hoodie.

BOC! BOC!

As everyone jumped back in fear and surprise, D-Wub slid his gaze over the room and politely asked, "Does anyone else wish to be excused from the table?" After a moment of silence, he waved his gun at Gator's corpse and smirked, "Somebody give Blood a ride over to Swan Creek."

* * *

"That nigga Kool-Aid was a rat," D-Wub informed Boob-Mac and Suge in a disgusted tone as he flicked ashes onto the floor.

Their eyebrows rose in genuine shock. Now they understood the reason for his paranoia.

"That bitch-ass nigga ain't beat that fed case at no suppression hearin'. He took the stand on a nigga from the 'Nati and gave 'im a elbow."

They stared at D-Wub in disbelief, unable to presently comprehend that someone they once idolized could have fallen so weak. And as they listened to him explain how this was info he stumbled across just days ago, they noticed a look in D-Wub's eyes that made them suddenly suspect that they were in the presence of the man responsible for the still-unsolved murder. The same man who had attended Kool-Aid's funeral and held his baby momma in one arm, and infant son in the other.

"Enough about Master Splinter," D-Wub said, waving his hand dismissively. "'Cause that ain't even my main reason for being here. I just couldn't allow two good men to mourn the death of a fuck-nigga."

Grunting in mild pain, he then rose from the table and limped over to the sink, where he took a long pull off the cancer stick before putting it down the drain. *I'm killin' that nigga Juan-Juan first chance I get*, he thought angrily as he popped a Pere and washed it down with tap water.

"Niggas like us wasn't fortunate enough to ride the elevator," D-Wub began as he walked back to the table. "We was forced to take the stairs. So, shid, when we do catch blessings, we obligated to treat that mu'fucka like it might be our last." With that being said, he reached into the duffel bag and pulled out a brick of China. Watching their eyes instantly light up, he laid it on the table and continued, "I found this hidden in one of the nigga Kool-Aid's spots. So, y'all already know what we gotta do. Bust this bitch down and go gram-fa-gram."

Hungrily eyeing the scorpion-stamped package, they eagerly bobbed their heads in agreement. Since Kool-Aid's death, shit had been slower than an infant turtle. Now they were suddenly staring at an easy buck-fifty to $200,000.

"As far as Mook and 'nem," D-Wub continued, speaking in reference to the others on their team, "I'ma just have to make sho' they well-fed once I find a plug. But until then, shid, you niggas know the meaning of self-preservation." Then, with a crooked grin, he added, "An' you know the summer comin' up."

Boob-Mac flashed a mouthful of diamond-studded golds as he reached out and gave him the Blood shake. "I'ma put Forgi's on a Foreign!"

All eyes were now on Suge, who wore a slight frown as he continued to stare at the slab.

"Speak yo' mind, Gotti," D-Wub urged him.

Slowly shaking his head, he answered quietly, "I ain't wit' it, Wub."

Boob-Mac balled his face up. "You ain't wit' it? Nigga—"

D-Wub got his attention and silenced him with a firm head shake. He then turned back to Suge and studied him with a piercing stare. "So, that's how you feel?"

Knowing there would likely be consequences for his rebellion, he stood his ground. "That's how I feel, Gotti. I just can't see myself holdin' out on the same niggas I done been in them trenches wit'."

D-Wub drew his pistol with the speed of a cowboy in an old-western movie and squeezed.

BOK!

As blood began to leak from a hole in Boob-Mac's cheek, he looked at Suge and said, "He ain't loyal! Any nigga willing to hold out on his day ones can't be trusted."

After drenching the entire downstairs in gasoline- including Boob-Mac's body, they sent the house up in flames, then slid off in the 'Vette, bumping Yo Gotti. *"I ain't soft on these hoes... I ain't crossin' my folks. Feds come and scoop me, my mouth stayin' closed. 'Cause I'ma die a real nigga."*

* * *

Arriving in Columbus, Ohio, two hours later, JBo steered them to a studio apartment on the city's north side. For $3,000 cash and nothing in writing, it was theirs for a month.

Aside from mourning the loss of Olivia, JBo had managed to get everything set up during his two-week disappearance. He had disassembled the Hyundai and removed what they had bought from Bobby-Ray down in West-V. The on-line orders and everything else needed was already stashed inside the apartment, and both cars had been delivered from Rocky's to a nearby storage unit.

When they stepped inside the apartment, JBo noticed the way T-Woods and Ham were staring at the four air-mattresses in the front room. Placing a hand on T-Woods' shoulder, he shrugged. "The less privacy, the better."

After smashing three oven-baked pizzas and blowing a stick of Fruity, they crawled their exhausted bodies into the make-shift beds and passed out.

* * *

The following morning, the four men were huddled around the kitchen table as JBo explained the lick from A-to-Z. There was a large diagram on the table of a building, its parking lot, and several escape routes. "So, after we go back to the storage and switch cars, we gon' shoot down to Marion—a small white town thirty-minutes away—where I already got four other cars wit' full tanks and GPS. We split the money, then spread out over the map. Nobody knowing where nobody else goin'."

T-Woods bobbed his head in approval as he blew a Kush cloud toward the ceiling. "Yeah, this shit sound official." He could already visualize himself coming through the west side of Cleveland in a snow-white Jag.

After rehearsing their roles for several more hours, they paused for a lunch break and went to a Steak-n-Shake not far from the apartment. While in the drive-thru waiting on their orders, JBo casually nudged his head at the front windshield. "That's the one we runnin' up in tomorrow," he said in reference to a glass building directly across the street.

Back at the apartment, JBo opened up a barber shop in the kitchen, with T-Woods being his first customer.

"Nigga, you 'bout to look like a cold creep," Ham joked as he began shaving off his beard.

JBo had to snatch the clippers back from T-Woods' face as they fell out laughing.

An awkward silence came over the room when it was Juan-Juan's turn. He reluctantly walked into the kitchen and took a seat; his expression making it clear he was not in the mood for jokes. He closed his eyes as JBo grabbed one of his beloved shoulder-length plats and sawed it off. This would be his first time in life not having hair.

Later that night, with T-Woods behind the wheel, the four darkly-clothed men climbed into the Yukon and took a trip downtown. A satchel was slung over

JBo's shoulder as he and Ham hopped out on High Street and quickly dissolved into the darkness.

Twenty-minutes later, they were driving back to the apartment to cover last minute details.

Tomorrow was Game 7, leaving no room for error.

CHAPTER 21
8AM The Following Morning

Wearing latex gloves and stone-faced expressions, the four men hastily exited the apartment, carrying six large duffel bags. Before leaving, they had sanitized the apartment until it was cleaner than a children's hospital.

Silence was the only sound inside the truck as JBo drove southbound on High Street, for each man understood that it would soon boil down to only one of two possible outcomes— sink or swim.

When they got within the vicinity of downtown, JBo turned onto a one-way side street and parked in the center of the block. He scanned his mirrors before giving T-Woods a single head nod.

Using an untraceable cellphone, he punched in a number and hit send.

"Nine-one-one, what is your emergency?"

"Listen carefully," he began in a practiced southern drawl, "we tied of the po-lice killin' us and gettin' away wit' it. So, today the day we fight back."

As soon as he disconnected the call, JBo began dialing a series of memorized numbers on a Motorola flip. He pressed the green display, listened for a second, then hung up and started dialing a different number. Unconsciously holding his breath, he hesitated a split-second before pressing send.

* * *

Columbus Police Station

Known for his sense of humor among his own kind, Officer Matthew Warwick held everyone's attention as he told a joke. "So, this plane is in the sky when it suddenly starts to go down. When they figure out it's because the plane is too heavy, they start throwing off the animals. When that doesn't work, they start throwing off luggage. When that still wasn't enough, the pilot decides that they'll have to start throwing off people. So, he comes over the intercom and says he'll keep it fair by going in alphabetical order. He says, 'Are there any African Americans on this plane?' When no one speaks up, a little girl looks up at her mother and says, 'Momma, ain't we African American?' The woman quickly shakes her head. 'Are there any Blacks on this plane?' the pilot asks. After a minute of silence, the little girl looks back up at her mother. 'Momma ain't we Black?' Again, the woman shakes her head and signals for her daughter to be quiet. 'Are there any Coloreds on this plane?' the pilot then asks. After no one says anything this time, the little girl frowns in confusion as she looks back up at her mother. 'Momma ain't we Colored?' The woman shakes her head as she leans down and whispers, 'Today we some Niggers.'"

As the officers roared in laughter, Gary Owens— a black detective— grunted in disgust as he got up to leave.

"Aw come on, Gary," Warwick called out after him. "It was just a—"

BOOOOOOOMMMMM!

His words were cut short as the building was suddenly rocked by a deafening explosion. In a matter of seconds, the first floor was literally disintegrated while the entire upstairs had collapsed. Amid the stifling smoke, piles of rubble, and charred flesh, there were no survivors.

When the explosion was heard inside the Yukon, T-Woods hit redial.

"Nine-one-one, what is your emergency?"

"The prosecutor's offices next." Disconnecting the call, he cracked his door open, then leaned down and dropped both phones into the opening of a storm drain.

JBo calmly threw the truck in drive and eased away from the curb, en route to the storage unit.

When T-Woods had dropped JBo and Ham off downtown the night before, the two men had nervously snuck to the back of the police station. With Ham holding a small flashlight, JBo had quickly sat the bag on the ground and removed ten pounds of C-4. Sticking two five-pound blocks to the building, he inserted a detonator into both, then crept around front and did the same.

According to the instructions provided by Bobby-Ray, the explosives operated on two mechanisms: activation and detonation. The first number JBo had dialed caused a red light to appear on all four detonators, signaling activation. When he made the second call, the red lights turned green, blinked twice, then all four blocks had detonated simultaneously. It was a well-spent $25,000.

As soon as they drove up to their storage unit, everyone wordlessly sprung into action. T-Woods and Juan-Juan backed the cars out and quickly began unloading the truck. Ham screwed phony tags to both cars, while JBo ran a hand-held vacuum over the truck's interior. Satisfied that he had left no hair follicles or other DNA behind, he jumped in with T-Woods and the two cars fled the scene.

Five minutes later, they were turning into the parking lot of the glass building. With it being just a quarter-till-nine, there were only a few other cars present.

Having no time to spare, JBo cut his eyes at T-Woods as they replaced their latex gloves for leather ones. "You ready?"

CHAPTER 22

"I need everyone's attention!" T-Woods barked with authority as he and JBo marched into the PNC bank. Official-looking in a replica police uniform, he continued, "My name is Officer Keith Hightower with the Columbus Police Department, and standing next to me is Special Agent Steven Grant from the Federal Bureau of Investigation."

Rocking a navy-blue suit, soft-soled dress shoes, and brown contacts, JBo stepped forward and flashed an authentic-looking badge. "If I could please have everyone present, front and center. The Bureau has just received classified intelligence that this bank is the target of a wanted and extremely dangerous crew of bank robbers." He and T-Woods inwardly smiled as the employees scurried in their direction. "Is this everyone?" JBo questioned the five people fearfully standing before him.

When their heads bobbed in unison, he and T-Woods swiftly withdrew their firearms and ordered them to get on their knees and reach for the ceiling.

As they slowly complied with confused expressions, T-Woods relieved the security guard of his weapon and smiled. "Wouldn't want you to hurt anybody."

JBo squatted in front of a chubby white man who he already knew was the bank's manager. "Seeing your family again is more important than the money in this bank."

His jaws jiggled as he quickly nodded in agreement.

Taking one hand off his gun, T-Woods grabbed the walkie-talkie clipped to his shirt and spoke into it. "Oh-six-oh to Oh-six-oh, it's a go."

"Copy."

A minute later, Juan-Juan and Ham—both wearing Oakley sport sunglasses and police uniforms— entered the bank with the duffel bags.

In his preparing for the lick, JBo had thought to do a number of things that would help disguise their true identities. From changing their skin color with make-up, to phony facial hair, contact lenses, and even a pair of customized shoes that made Ham appear several inches taller. As a result, the cameras in and outside the bank would record four men who didn't exist.

After locking the front door, they ushered the employees into a back room, where everyone besides the manager was bound, gagged and made to lie face down.

While T-Woods held the manager at gunpoint, Juan-Juan went and stood over the security guard and fired two shots into the back of his skull.

BOK! BOK!

At witnessing the cold-blooded execution, the manager squeezed his eyes shut as he cringed in fear.

The message sent, Juan-Juan and JBo then picked up the bags and followed behind T-Woods as he roughly led the manager from the room.

Pausing in the doorway, JBo turned back to face Ham. "You know what to do."

He forced himself not to smile as he looked down at the employees and nodded. "I got it." His job was to search for and seize any cellphones or electronic devices found, then post up at the front entrance and inform anyone who arrived that the bank was closed until further notice. But Ham being Ham, he had other ideas.

When T-Woods shoved the manager into the vault's circular-shaped door, JBo walked up behind him and calmly spoke into his ear, "You only get one shot. So, think about the family."

He nodded, then lifted a trembling hand and slowly moved it over the key-pad.

After several intense and breath-holding seconds, the locks disengaged and the manager opened the 1,000-pound door and stepped aside.

A level of excitement impossible to explain overcame the three men as they stared in at a room full of money. *We rich!*

While the bombing of the police station appeared to be retaliation for the countless Blacks slain by the hands of racist cops, its primary reason had been to create a diversion. As every law enforcement agency known to man would respond to the downtown scene to search for possible survivors, they would also have to deal with the courthouse. Having no idea it was an empty threat, they would have to evacuate the entire building and call in the bomb squad.

Meanwhile, on the opposite side of town, four armed bandits would have more than enough time to raid the vault of a PNC bank.

After having the manager warn them on which bills to avoid, they tied him up and gagged him, then quickly began stuffing the bags with fifties and hundreds only. In under three minutes they had the money loaded onto a pushcart and were hauling ass.

As they rounded the corner and entered the front lobby, they immediately noticed something that made them stop dead in their tracks.

Ham was nowhere in sight.

Eyes blazing with anger, JBo spun on T-Woods. "Go see where that clown at!"

Jogging back to the room they had left him in, he went to step through the doorway and froze in disbelief. With his gun pointed at the head of a voluptuous older white woman, Ham held a fistful of her hair while forcing his dick in and out of her mouth.

As T-Woods reached for his strap in disgust, he felt a presence behind him and turned.

BOK!

His heart stopped before he dropped.

When Ham looked over his shoulder, his eyes widened right before Juan-Juan squeezed again.

BOK!

The woman shrieked in terror as she scooted to a far corner of the room.

Juan-Juan gave T-Woods another one as he stepped over his body, then walked down on Ham, who was on the floor, clutching his hands to his neck in a desperate attempt to suppress the steady flow of blood. Without flinching, he stared him in his terrified eyes and fired twice.

BOK! BOK!

In no hurry, he calmly swiveled on his heels and left the room.

As if it was a normal procedure, Juan-Juan held open the bank's front door as JBo rolled the cart out. He then ran ahead and popped the trunks to both cars.

Prior to the lick, they had decided that it would be unwise to haul all the money in one car.

"See you in Marion," JBo said as he slammed his trunk.

Juan-Juan nodded, the look in his eyes hidden behind the mirrored sunglasses.

Inside the Ford Taurus, JBo stuck a Black and Mild between his lips and watched as Juan-Juan pulled off. *We did it!* He rejoiced to himself as he dug in his pocket for a light.

Compliments of Rocky, their cars bore the look of law enforcement vehicles. The Taurus, with its souped-up engine, was all black with light tint and phony government tags. And the charger had a wrap-job with overhead strobe-lights that made it appear nearly identical to one of the cruisers driven by the police department. Besides having to leave T-Woods and Ham behind, it had been a well-executed plan.

"Bitch!" JBo swore as the lighter fell between the seat. Leaning forward, he felt around until he found it, then sparked the cigar and took a soothing pull. As he went to bring the engine to life, his eyes instinctively glanced up at the rear-view mirror.

His worst fear suddenly came to life as his heart started pounding against his chest. A real cop car was sitting right behind him.

Although JBo could only blame himself, his present dilemma was actually the result of Ham's foolishness. By not playing his role, the woman he sexually assaulted had been able to chew off one of her co-workers' wrist restraints; allowing her to dial 911 and scream for help.

Traveling from a nearby county, two police officers—Keaton and McDonald—were on their way to the frantic scene downtown when the dispatch came over the radio, reporting a deadly bank robbery in progress. With sixteen courageous years of experience under their belts, the duo didn't hesitate to follow the motto engraved on their badges—to protect and serve.

As the Hemi left its signature on the pavement, Officer Keaton anxiously un-holstered his service weapon and thumbed off the safety.

When they cautiously wheeled into the bank's parking lot, their watchful eyes had spotted a person's silhouette inside the dark colored sedan with government tags. Taking no chances, they ran the plate number. When it came back as non-existent, they called for back-up, then went straight into go-mode.

Using their car doors as cover, the two veterans quickly hopped out and aimed their Sigs at the Taurus.

Without taking his eyes off the car, Keaton grabbed a mic from the center console and spoke over the intercom, "Driver, lower your window and slowly place both hands out with your palms up!"

Juan-Juan was a safe distance away when he heard over the scanner what was taking place back at the bank. Displaying no physical reaction, he unplugged the scanner and offered a silent apology to JBo, for him getting caught up was something he had already known would happen. It was one of the parts in his dream he had been keeping secret all along.

See you on the other side, my nigga, he thought sadly as he switched lanes and hit his right turn signal.

Cursing himself for allowing his addiction to override common sense, JBo teared up. With no choice but to accept the consequences of his costly mistake, he lowered his window, then took a long pull off the cigar before flicking it out onto the pavement. Images of Olivia flashed before him as he grabbed his Glock and racked one in the chamber.

His hand on the door handle, JBo was a split-second from making his move when another cop car suddenly sped into the parking lot. Making a wide turn, the driver swung the car around until his grill was pointed directly at JBo's door. His eyes bulged in disbelief when the officer boldly jumped out and ran down on him with both hands gripping his firearm.

"Pull off!" Juan-Juan ordered in a harsh whisper.

JBo eyed him in confusion. "Pull off?"

"You got three seconds to put this bitch in drive, or I'ma put you down myself." While it hurt Juan-Juan to speak to him in such a manner, it was the only way.

"What is you doin', my nigga?"

He cocked the hammer back. "One... two..."

As JBo reluctantly turned the ignition and put the car in drive, Juan-Juan pivoted toward the cop car and opened fire.

BOK! BOK! BOK! BOK! BOK! BOK! BOK! BOK!

Scrambling to the back of their car, McDonald snatched the walkie-talkie off his shirt. "Officers under fire! I repeat, officers under fire!"

Using their fear to his advantage, Juan-Juan grabbed a bag off the backseat of the Charger and raced to the front of a SRT8 Jeep Cherokee. With the cop car still in his sights, he crouched down then raised his gun and patiently waited.

When McDonald nervously risked a peek from behind the car, Juan-Juan ended his life with a Hydro-shock above the left eyebrow. He would leave behind a wife and two kids.

In a fit of rage, Officer Keaton came up blazing.
BLOOM! BLOOM! BLOOM! BLOOM! BLOOM! BLOOM! BLOOM!

Juan-Juan watched in amusement as he shattered the Charger's windows and Swiss-cheesed the exterior. Just as he was about to return fire, his instincts made him turn around.

He found himself staring into the saddened eyes of JBo, who had exited the parking lot and was slowly driving away. Their intense gaze held a mixture of emotions as both men understood that this was it. There would be no more Juan-Juan and JBo.

Unable to see the tears that fell from JBo's eyes, Juan-Juan balled up his fist and banged it over his heart; imitating JBo when he had fought Kool-Aid at St. Mary's. It was his way of saying goodbye, for he was on the verge of offering the most ultimate sacrifice himself. This was the final part of his dream he had been keeping secret.

Their connection was broken as reinforcements swarmed the parking lot. Using their cars as shields, they leveled their guns at the Charger and ordered Juan-Juan to surrender.

Ignoring the warning, he stared after JBo's taillights until they were no longer visible. *I love you, my nigga.* He then reached into the bag and exchanged the handgun for an AR-15 with a collapsible stock, where armor piercing bullets the size of bike-pegs huddled together inside the SO-round drum. He was not going alone.

"This is your final warning. Lay down your weapon and come out with your hands up!"

Without an inkling of fear within his heart, Juan-Juan click-clacked one in the head, then, with a fierce expression, came up squeezing. Slightly bucking in his arms, the rifle wreaked havoc as he sprayed in a sweeping motion while advancing toward them.

TAT! TAT! TAT! TAT! TAT! TAT! TAT! TAT! TAT! TAT! TAT! TAT!

The element of surprise allowed him to cut down four and critically wound several more before he caught one in the left shoulder. As the arm uselessly fell to his side, he braced the stock into the crook of his right arm and continued to squeeze.

Boldly stationed in the center of the parking lot, Juan-Juan staggered back as multiple shots punctured his vest. As he went to swing the AR in the shooter's direction, a hollow tore through his right bicep and forced him to drop the gun. He was then brought down to one knee when two more lodged themselves in his upper thigh. Bent over with one hand planted on the ground, the barely-healed wounds from several weeks ago, combined with today's had him dizzy with pain.

Not wanting to give the suspect the easy way out, the lead officer raised his hand as a signal to cease fire. He would find more pleasure in seeing the cop killer spend the rest of his life buried alive inside a 6 by 9 coffin.

As if Juan-Juan could read his mind, he gathered up every ounce of strength left in his body and lunged for the AR. By no means was going back an option.

While his body jerked in dance-like movements from their hail of bullets, he still managed to get off a few wild shots before he fell face-forward and kissed the pavement.

CHAPTER 23
24 Hours later

Ducked off inside an abandoned warehouse, JBo was still in a daze as he lay stretched out on the backseat of the Taurus. No matter how he looked at it, his weakness was the cause of Juan-Juan's demise. *Damn, my nigga*, he thought guiltily for the thousandth time. *I fucked up*. Knowing he could never touch another cigar, he crumpled the pack up and angrily flung it.

Already a day behind schedule, he glanced at his watch and knew it was time to move. He would have to mourn later.

Climbing out of the Taurus, he walked over to a 195 Buick Roadmaster and cranked it up. After transferring the money from one car to another, he was about to shut the Taurus's trunk when he saw something yellow lying off to the side. Picking it up out of curiosity, he unfolded the piece of paper and saw that it was addressed to him. With a look of confusion engraved on his face, he began to read.

JBo,

It ain't yo' fault, fam. I never told you my whole dream.

I left out the ending. I had to. We both know I'm beyond the point of savin'. I'm like deadweight slung over yo' shoulders, but because you a loyal soldier, you'll continue to carry me until yo' legs give out. And how can I continue to knowingly be the downfall of the only person that has ever loved me?

JBo had to look away from the letter as his vision became blurred by the tears forming in his eyes. He couldn't believe the depth of Juan-Juan's unselfish love. And while he subconsciously knew there was truth in his statements, he was too sad right then to accept it. If the hands of time could be reversed, he would have done so without a moment's hesitation.

* * *

An hour later, JBo was doing the speed limit on I-23 North. To minimize his chances of being pulled over, he was dressed like a Priest as he headed back to his hometown. At the end of his letter, Juan-Juan had asked him to act on his behalf before he got ghost. Because there was nothing linking him to crime scene, besides a known affiliation with one of the dead suspects, he knew he could safely slide in and out of the city.

Using a phony driver's license and passport, he would then get back on the road and drive to Mexico, where he had already reserved a flight through a private jet company. For $50,000 US, they offered an anonymous trip to anywhere in South America. With clearly over a million cash in his possession, he could easily start a new life; never again stepping foot back on US soil.

Arriving in Toledo two hours later, he pulled into a BP right off the E-way. With nearly two days of driving in store, he wanted to fill up the tank and grab a cup of straight-black. Then, after running the errand, he would jump right back on the road and put as much distance between himself and Ohio as possible.

With the coffee in hand, he left the gas station and avoided main roads as he navigated his way through the city's north side. Peering at the darkened streets from behind tinted windows, he shook his head in sympathy at the number of boarded-up houses, hoodie-wearing hooligans hungry for bodies, and hollow-face junkies scrambling for their next high.

Bending a left on Putnam, he eased up off the gas as he scanned the houses for the description Juan-Juan had written down. Not bothering to park, he braked in front of a deserted duplex and hit the horn. As he was about to hit it again, a shadowy figure cautiously appeared on the side of the house.

He lowered his window and yelled out, "Juan-Juan sent me!" When the man made no effort to come forward, he threw the car in park, then hit his hazards and hopped out. "He asked me to drop this off to you," JBo said as crossed the street with a bag held up in plain sight.

"Stop right there!" Terry Jones warned as reached inside his coat.

Unsure if he was bluffing or not, JBo paused. He had come too far to die at the hands of a damn bum. "I'ma just sit it right here on the ground, and you can grab it when I pull off."

Knowing Juan-Juan would never send anything harmful his way, Terry put aside his caution and came from between the houses, and asked, "He gone, huh?"

JBo nodded.

Already knowing the answer, he approached.

When Terry got within several feet, JBo froze up as his eyes widened in disbelief. After fantasizing about this day for years, he was finally standing face-to-face with his mother's killer.

To Be Continued...
The Cost of Loyalty 2
Coming Soon

Submission Guideline.

Submit the first three chapters of your completed manuscript to ldpsubmissions@gmail.com, subject line: Your book's title. The manuscript must be in a .doc file and sent as an attachment. Document should be in Times New Roman, double spaced and in size 12 font. Also, provide your synopsis and full contact information. If sending multiple submissions, they must each be in a separate email.

Have a story but no way to send it electronically? You can still submit to LDP/Ca$h Presents. Send in the first three chapters, written or typed, of your completed manuscript to:

LDP: Submissions Dept
Po Box 870494
Mesquite, Tx 75187

DO NOT send original manuscript. Must be a duplicate.

Provide your synopsis and a cover letter containing your full contact information.

Thanks for considering LDP and Ca$h Presents.

<u>Coming Soon from Lock Down Publications/Ca$h Presents</u>

BOW DOWN TO MY GANGSTA

By **Ca$h**

TORN BETWEEN TWO

By **Coffee**

BLOOD STAINS OF A SHOTTA **III**

By **Jamaica**

WHEN THE STREETS CLAP BACK **III**

By **Jibril Williams**

STEADY MOBBIN

By **Marcellus Allen**

BLOOD OF A BOSS **V**

By **Askari**

THE HEART OF A GANGSTA **III**

By **Jerry Jackson**

LOYAL TO THE GAME **IV**

By **T.J. & Jelissa**

A DOPEBOY'S PRAYER **II**

By **Eddie "Wolf" Lee**

IF LOVING YOU IS WRONG… **III**

LOVE ME EVEN WHEN IT HURTS

By **Jelissa**

DAUGHTERS OF A SAVAGE

By **Chris Green**

BLOODY COMMAS **III**

SKI MASK CARTEL **II**

The Cost of Loyalty

By **T.J. Edwards**

TRAPHOUSE KING

By **Hood Rich**

BLAST FOR ME **II**

RAISED AS A GOON **V**

By **Ghost**

A DISTINGUISHED THUG STOLE MY HEART **III**

By **Meesha**

ADDICTIED TO THE DRAMA **III**

By **Jamila Mathis**

LIPSTICK KILLAH **II**

By **Mimi**

THE BOSSMAN'S DAUGHTERS **IV**

WHAT BAD BITCHES DO

By **Aryanna**

The Cost of Loyalty **II**

By **Kweli**

A Drug King and His Diamond **II**

By **Nicole Goosby**

Available Now

RESTRAINING ORDER **I & II**

By **CA$H & Coffee**

LOVE KNOWS NO BOUNDARIES **I II & III**

By **Coffee**

RAISED AS A GOON I, II, III & IV

BRED BY THE SLUMS I, II, III

BLAST FOR ME

By **Ghost**

LAY IT DOWN **I & II**

LAST OF A DYING BREED

BLOOD STAINS OF A SHOTTA I & II

By **Jamaica**

LOYAL TO THE GAME

LOYAL TO THE GAME II

LOYAL TO THE GAME III

By **TJ & Jelissa**

BLOODY COMMAS I & II

SKI MASK CARTEL

By **T.J. Edwards**

IF LOVING HIM IS WRONG…I & II

By **Jelissa**

WHEN THE STREETS CLAP BACK

By **Jibril Williams**

A DISTINGUISHED THUG STOLE MY HEART I & II

By **Meesha**

PUSH IT TO THE LIMIT

By **Bre' Hayes**

BLOOD OF A BOSS **I, II, III & IV**

By **Askari**

THE STREETS BLEED MURDER **I, II & III**

THE HEART OF A GANGSTA I & II

By **Jerry Jackson**

CUM FOR ME

The Cost of Loyalty

Kweli

By **Frank Gresham**

THESE NIGGAS AIN'T LOYAL **I, II & III**

By **Nikki Tee**

GANGSTA SHYT **I II &III**

By **CATO**

THE ULTIMATE BETRAYAL

By **Phoenix**

BOSS'N UP **I , II & III**

By **Royal Nicole**

I LOVE YOU TO DEATH

By Destiny J

I RIDE FOR MY HITTA

I STILL RIDE FOR MY HITTA

By **Misty Holt**

LOVE & CHASIN' PAPER

By **Qay Crockett**

TO DIE IN VAIN

By **ASAD**

BROOKLYN HUSTLAZ

By **Boogsy Morina**

BROOKLYN ON LOCK I & II

By **Sonovia**

GANGSTA CITY

By **Teddy Duke**

A DRUG KING AND HIS DIAMOND

A DOPEMAN'S RICHES

By Nicole Goosby

BOOKS BY LDP'S CEO, CA$H

TRUST IN NO MAN

TRUST IN NO MAN 2

TRUST IN NO MAN 3

BONDED BY BLOOD

SHORTY GOT A THUG

THUGS CRY

THUGS CRY 2

THUGS CRY 3

TRUST NO BITCH

TRUST NO BITCH 2

TRUST NO BITCH 3

TIL MY CASKET DROPS

RESTRAINING ORDER

RESTRAINING ORDER 2

IN LOVE WITH A CONVICT

Coming Soon

BONDED BY BLOOD 2

BOW DOWN TO MY GANGSTA

Kweli

CPSIA information can be obtained
at www.ICGtesting.com
Printed in the USA
LVHW04s1441210518
577952LV00011B/1072/P